MW00936232

Darcy's Continental Escape

Melanie Schertz

Copyright © 2016 Melanie Schertz

All rights reserved.

ISBN: 1532713886
ISBN-13: 9781532713880

DEDICATION

This story is dedicated to my friends and family, near and far, who have been the wind beneath my wings. Thank you for your support and love.
And to my friend, Annie, from Germany, who has helped me make this as authentic as possible when it came to places and events. I am grateful for your assistance and your friendship.

CONTENTS

ACKNOWLEDGMENTS

I am grateful to Wikipedia, and other sites that have given me the historical information that is in my story. Most of the places mentioned in the story are real and the history was gleaned from the internet . So much incredible history that was amazing to learn about, including the King's German Legion. There are actually copies of journals written by men involved in the Legion, over 200 years ago, telling about their lives and battles.

Thank you to Jane Austen, for the loving characters that you gave us, who are like old friends who are a part of us.

And thank you to all my friends and fellow authors in the JAFF community. You are an amazing group of people, and have blessed my life in so many wonderful ways.

CHAPTER 1

April 1809

"Mother, we must make haste." Richard Fitzwilliam called to his mother.

Klarissa Fitzwilliam, nee Adler, was speaking to her maid about the packing of her trunks. "I am telling Alice what needs to be packed in which trunk. It is important, as to ensure there is no damage."

"Your clothing is not going to matter if you are killed. Tell your maid to pack a few items in a satchel and let us be off."

"Nonsense. There is plenty of time to do things properly. My sister would have told us if there is a need to hurry." The Countess of Matlock had brought her younger son and her nephew on holiday on the continent, as they had both graduated from the university in England. The Countess was originally from Austria, and it had been years since she had last visited her homeland. Her sister, Arabelle, was married to a politician, which made Lady Matlock feel no rush in evacuating their townhouse in Vienna, where they had been staying for the previous three months. "With your uncle's position, he would be one of the first to learn of an invasion."

"Aunt Klarissa, Richard and I were down by the Danube. We overheard men speaking of French troops moving on Vienna. We need to leave immediately. Any delay could be dangerous for all of us." Fitzwilliam Darcy, the only nephew of Lord and Lady Matlock, stated. "You should leave your belongings with your sister, and she can send them to you when everything is settled down."

"I do not wish to leave them behind. What of the beautiful set of dishes that were my mother's? What if something happened to them? Mother left them to me, when she died last year."

"Please, Mother, Grandmama would not wish for you to be harmed just to bring her dishes with us. She would tell you to flee as quickly as possible." Richard was frustrated with his mother's attitude. He had been preparing to join the Army upon his return to England, and his senses were sharp for the coming battle. "If we hurry, we can be on one of the ships that will sail up on the Danube. Once we are safely away from here, we can make our way towards Hamburg. With your being fluent in languages, we will be able to blend in better, not appearing to be British."

They heard the front door of the house open and someone entering quickly. The sound of one of the footmen stepping towards his Mistress' study was obvious. Richard and Darcy looked at each other for a moment, then hurried to follow the footman. Lady Matlock had to admit that it was highly unusual for a servant to behave in such a manner.

As they reached the open door of the study, Arabelle came hurrying to find them. "Sister, you must leave immediately. I just received word that the French are entering the city. Please, you must go now."

"But...but..." Lady Matlock was shocked.

"No time for delays, you must hurry. Richard, come. Your uncle left me with a map and papers, as a precaution. He was certain that Napoleon would arrive, just not so soon. Take all these papers, they should keep you safe. Prepare yourselves for leaving. Please, Klarissa, take only a few clothes. I will have the cook prepare a basket for you. But you must hurry."

Finally, Lady Matlock felt fear. She knew, by the look in her sister's eyes, that it would be dangerous to remain, especially if the enemy learned they were British. Richard and Darcy could be killed.

They hurried and packed a single satchel each. Arabelle came to the front door to farewell them, handing Richard a basket containing food for the trio.

Arabelle gave her sister a quick embrace and a kiss on the cheek. "Safe journey, Klarissa. Take care of the boys."

Richard chuckled lightly at his aunt's use of the word boys. "Yes, Mother, you must keep us *boys* safe."

Arabelle smiled as she gave her nephew a slight swat on his arm. "You know what I mean, Richard. You and Fitzwilliam keep your mother safe."

"We will." Darcy answered for them both.

Within minutes, the trio were out the door and heading towards the docks of the river. They moved quickly, not wishing to be captured by Napoleon's troops.

~~ ** ~~

"Lizzy, you and Adam must hurry." Randolph Gardiner declared, as he attempted to speed his niece and nephew from his home. "Jacqueline says you must make haste. Her brother is an officer, and he said it is not safe here for you."

Mr Gardiner had lived in Vienna for nearly twenty years. He had met and married a young lady named Gretchen, and Jacqueline was a cousin of Gretchen's family. The young lady came to tend the house for Mr Gardiner, who was alone after his wife's death two years previously. Mr Gardiner was the eldest brother of Mrs Fanny Bennet, the mother of Elizabeth and Alex Bennet. The Bennet family consisted of six children and their parents. Alex , Jane, Elizabeth, Mary, Katherine, and Lydia were adored by their parents, and they lived on their father's estate of Longbourn, in Hertfordshire, in England.

Alex had recently graduated from Oxford, and his uncle had invited the young man to visit him in Vienna, and spend some time with his relations. Knowing how dear such a trip would be for his second born sister, Elizabeth, Alex persuaded his father to allow her to join him on the holiday. Alex was one and twenty, and his sister was nine and ten. Mr Bennet felt safe in allowing the two to travel without a parent, and he was certain all was safe, since the Treaty of Pressburg in 1805, all had been quiet, according to Mr Gardiner.

The Bennet children had arrived at their uncle's home in February. They were originally supposed to remain with him for another three months, but the impending battle changed their plans. Mr Gardiner knew of other cities and villages that had been attacked by the French army, which left him full of fear for his nephew and niece.

Alex looked at his uncle. "Please, you must come with us. You are English, the French will kill you."

"My dear boy, I have no desire to leave here. This is where I lived with my beloved wife. My memories fill this home, and my wife's spirit is in every corner of the home. No, I will not leave. And if it is my time to make my final journey, I will be reunited with my dear Gretchen. But you and Lizzy must leave, and quickly."

Mr Gardiner assisted the pair to the docks on the Danube. He had told them the best route to take, suggesting that their best chance at reaching home would be to travel to Hamburg. From there, they could make their way back to England.

The trio bid their farewells, and Mr Gardiner herded the brother and sister towards a line of people preparing to board a ship.

"Safe journey, Alex. Safe journey, Lizzy. Give your family my best."

"Goodbye Uncle." The pair declared in unison.

Mr Gardiner moved back from his relations, though decided to watch until the ship sailed before he left.

As the line moved forward, Elizabeth and Alex had finally reached the gangplank. Suddenly, there were shouts and screams coming from the city, sounds of gunfire and frightened people. People on the dock began to push and shove to gain the deck of the ship. Alex attempted to protect his sister, keeping her in front of him. The sound of gunfire was coming closer, and the panic stricken people became frantic. The pushing and shoving grew worse, and some of the men behind Alex and Elizabeth began fighting.

Two ladies and one man were knocked from the gangplank and they fell into the water. The struggle continued, and Alex had to protect his sister. Elizabeth was on the ship, and Alex had one foot on the deck, when the fight to escape the city grew worse. One of the men had pulled out a gun and began shooting people. Elizabeth was holding her brother's hand, when he seemed to be slipping backwards from her. Turning around, she looked into his eyes. There was a look of fear and pain etched in his eyes, eyes that normally sparkled with delight. Then she saw the blood blossoming on his chest. He had been shot. Blood began to run from the corner of his mouth, down his chin.

As he was falling backwards, pulling Elizabeth with him, Elizabeth knew her beloved brother was already gone. The life that usually shone from him had completely disappeared from him. She wished she could die as well. "Alex …Please, Alex. Someone help my brother. He has been wounded."

Just as Elizabeth was about to tumble over from the ship, two young men took hold of her. They pulled her back, as Alex's hand slipped from hers and plummeted to the water below. Elizabeth struggled against the hands that were holding her. A moment later, the gangplank was knocked loose from the ship, falling into the water, along with several other people.

"Let me go. I must go back for my brother." Elizabeth cried. The ship had begun to move from the dock, and she could not reach her brother.

"I am truly sorry, Miss. Your brother is gone. The injury he suffered was fatal." One of the men stated.

"My cousin is correct. Please, you cannot go back. He is dead."

"Alex … Alex …my dear brother. It cannot be true. He is a strong man, he will be able to survive, if given proper care. My uncle lives there; he will know a surgeon. Please, I must return."

A woman's voice spoke soothingly. "If you were to go back, you as well would be killed. Would your brother wish for you to be killed, or raped? For the

French will take advantage of you. We will look after you. My son and nephew are good men, and they will protect us from harm."

Elizabeth was sobbing as she turned into the arms of the lady. "My brother...he is a good man...and now he is gone."

"My poor dear girl, this is a terrible time. Now, let us find someplace to sit. There are so many people on the ship, but we will find somewhere. Then we can talk further."

Elizabeth was escorted to the compartment which was used for many purposes, though primarily, for dining. She did not know what was happening, all she could remember was the look in her brother's eyes as he fell away from her, dropping into the water. Though she had seen everything, she could not make herself believe that her brother was dead. And now she was alone. It was too painful to accept.

The woman who had guided her into the room spoke. "My name is Klarissa Fitzwilliam, Countess of Matlock. These young men are my younger son, Richard Fitzwilliam, and my nephew, Fitzwilliam Darcy. Might I inquire as to your name?"

Several minutes passed before Elizabeth was able to comprehend what the woman had said. "I...I...am Elizabeth Bennet, of Longbourn, in Hertfordshire."

"And the young man, he was your brother?" Darcy inquired. He hated to cause her any further pain, but he wished to know more about the Bennets.

"My older brother, Alex. I left him. I just left him. Alex must think quite ill of me. I must return, as our father gave me explicit instructions to do as my brother told me and stay close to him. Here I am, with people I do not know, while my brother is injured and so far from me."

Darcy kneeled before Elizabeth. "Miss Bennet, I am afraid your brother did not survive his injuries. He was shot through the chest. As much as it pains me to say this, your brother is dead."

Elizabeth searched his eyes for the truth. Deep in her heart, she knew he was correct, but it was too painful to accept. But her eyes pleaded for him to say that her brother would recover and be on his way to join her soon.

"It is my fault. Alex insisted I walk in front of him. If I had been behind him, he would have been safe. I should have died, not Alex. He is all that is lgood and kind, just as my elder sister, Jane. My family will be devastated. I want to die."

"Miss Bennet, this is no way for a young lady to behave." Lady Matlock said. "Would your brother think you are behaving as a proper young lady? Is this paying respect to your brother, who did all that he could to protect you? He would not wish for you to die, I am certain. Any brother who would protect their sister, as yours did, would not wish to see her die. I am certain that he would have been broken hearted to hear you speak in such a manner."

More tears fell from Elizabeth's eyes. "I do not wish to dishonor my brother. He has always been so good to me."

"Then it is time to dry those tears, hold your head up, and thank God that your brother has given you a chance at life. Do not throw away his sacrifice."

Elizabeth nodded, as she reached in her reticule, looking for her handkerchief. Then a hand was before her, holding one out to her. She looked up into the eyes of a very kind Fitzwilliam Darcy. Accepting his offer, Elizabeth wiped her eyes, then placed the handkerchief in her pocket. "I will have it laundered for you as soon as I can, Mr Darcy."

"I have others, Miss Bennet. You may keep it as long as you wish."

"Many thanks to you, Mr Darcy. And for attempting to catch my brother, before he fell. And thanks to you, Mr Fitzwilliam, for your assistance."

Richard gave her a sad smile. "You have my

deepest regrets for your loss, Miss Bennet. We will do all that we can to protect you and see that you are returned home to your loved ones."

~~ ** ~~

"We can disembark the ship at Krems, and make our way to Prague, then over to Hamburg." Richard and Darcy were examining the maps they had brought with them. "Or we can continue on the ship until we reach either Nuremberg or Bamberg, then head north to Hamburg. Prague might be safer, as it is further from the French, but I think we should take our chances and try to make it to Bamberg. We would be in Germany, but we have Mother who can speak for us, with her being fluent in the language." Richard stated.

"I do not like taking too many chances." Darcy replied.

"We are in an area where war has just broken out. So long as we avoid France itself, we should be able to pass ourselves off as natives. I believe it is best if we claim being one family, as it would less likely appear that we are on holiday. Mother, are you willing to claim Darcy as a son, and Miss Bennet as a daughter?"

Lady Matlock still held her arm around Elizabeth's shoulders, as the young lady was looking out the window of the room. "I have no difficulty with such deception. Miss Bennet, will you allow us to claim you as family, to protect you better?"

Elizabeth had not been paying close attention. "Forgive me, Lady Matlock, my mind was gathering wool. What did you say?"

"My son has suggested we claim to be a mother with her three children, to make us appear less like wealthy travelers on a holiday. What do you think?"

"I can see the wisdom in such a plan."

"Then it is no more Miss Bennet. You are Elizabeth, and I will be Mother. Richard and William will be your brothers. I know it is highly improper, but it will be safer this way. And we will need to find more appropriate clothing. Silks are not the custom of common folks. I should have heeded your advice, Richard. As much as I adore this gown, I will need to find something less ostentatious. And you boys, you should obtain some different clothing. William, your boots are far too shiny for a commoner. Wherever we disembark, we will need to find somewhere to do some shopping. Then we should purchase a carriage or wagon, and some horses. Fortunately, we exchanged enough coins when we arrived, we should be able to make our way home to England." Lady Matlock was used to ruling over her home in the city and on their family estate. The wife of an earl, she was used to taking charge and commanding people, like a general in the army.

All were in agreement, and Elizabeth stated her also having funds in her reticule. They decided to take the ship to Bamberg, then move north to Hamburg. After some time had passed, one of the men from the ship brought around some water for everyone to drink. He apologized for the lack of supplies. "We were not prepared for the hurried departure, so our supplies were not yet loaded on the ship. We will take on more when we are further from Vienna."

Lady Matlock nodded her head in understanding. "Sir, I would rather be alive than have waited for refreshments. We will be fine for the time being."

The man appreciated the kindness of the obviously wealthy family. Many others had looked offended when all he had to offer was water. To him, this was a family with class and character.

~~~~~~~ ** ~~~~~~~

Chapter 2

Most of the people who had boarded the ship were fleeing the invasion that was heading for Vienna. Scared women, terrified children, husbands wishing to protect their family. Some were Austrian, some German, and a few others were British.

After several hours, the man who had served water to everyone came over to Lady Matlock and her family. Speaking in German, he said. "Pardon me, but are you from England?"

"Yes." Lady Matlock replied, watching the man carefully.

"You are trying to return home, to England?"

Again, Lady Matlock affirmed.

"I heard the young men speaking. You will go to Bamberg?"

"That was what my sons were discussing. Might I ask why you wish to know?"

The man looked around, making certain that no one was listening in on the conversation. "My family, we wish to go to England. Too dangerous to remain here. My wife is English born. She could be killed if she stays. Our house is near Bamberg."

Lady Matlock was sure she understood for what the man wished, but she needed to make certain. "And you wish to travel with us?"

A nod was her reply. "We can protect you, help you find your way from here. All we ask in return is that you take us with you."

"As you can see, I can speak the language. What can you do for us?"

"My wife and I speak many languages. And my wife, she can cook. Our children are small; they will not be a bother. And we can assist you in finding the best route to take to get away from the French."

Curiosity took hold of Lady Matlock. "My sons have looked over the maps they brought with us. They know what would be the safest roads."

The man shook his head. "They may know what is on paper, but have they ever made the journey before? Lines on a piece of paper does not make the road safe. I have been in the area before. I am certain we will be able to keep you from harm."

Lady Matlock was suspicious, though, after a few moments of studying the man, she decided to trust him. "William, Richard, would you come to me?"

When the men stepped to Lady Matlock, they knelt beside her. Richard spoke. "Yes, Mother?"

"This is…"

The man realized he had not disclosed his name to the fine lady. "Dietrich, Dietrich Bauer."

"Mr Bauer wishes to assist us in our journey, if we are willing to assist him and his family to England." Lady Matlock stated softly. She did not wish for others to learn of the discussion.

Richard looked at his cousin before speaking. "Mr Bauer, why would we require your assistance?"

"You have no guide, only a map. As I said to your mother, lines on paper do not always tell the truth. Especially when the wars change the area quickly. I was born and raised in here. And I need to protect my family. My wife, Emily, was born in your country. If the French reach our home, my wife will be killed. All of our neighbors know of my wife's nationality, they would turn her in to save their own hides. We have children, they are young. I wish to protect my family, as you do yours. Between us, I believe we can all arrive in England."

Darcy spoke. "Tell us your suggestion."

"When we reach Bamberg, we will go ashore. My suggestion is for me to take you to the Michaelsberg Abbey. My cousin works there as a grounds keeper. He can keep you hidden. For your safety, it is best that we keep your being in the area quiet. Wealthy people attract attention. There are many who would not hesitate to rob you. Once at the Abbey, you will remain there. I will make the journey to my home, to have my wife prepare. Then, when I return to the Abbey, I will have my cousin make purchases for you, for clothes and food. The Abbey is no longer a monastery, it is an almshouse. His making the purchases will appear as though it is for the elderly who live there. After he returns, I will again go to my home, and load my wife and children on our wagon. It will not be a grand carriage, but it will get us where we need to go."

"And where is it we will need to go?" Darcy inquired.

"We would go across land, until we reach Cologne. From there, we can find passage on the Rhine River. The Rhine will take us where we need to go, leading to Amsterdam."

"If we are to take the Rhine, why not remain on the ship? Does this ship not go on the Main, which connects to the Rhine?" Darcy had studied the map thoroughly.

"Indeed. But if the French take the Danube, which is what they are likely after, how soon will they be coming this direction? There may be troops heading to the Danube from the south west. The Rhine comes up from the south to connect with the Main. The French can sail from Strasbourg, and be on their way to join those who have attacked Vienna. It is best to go on land, until we are far enough away from the war."

Richard was impressed. "You appear to have thought this through."

"Word reached us days ago that there could be trouble coming. The captain, he is thinking of making for the north. He suggested we all keep ready to flee from the French."

Lady Matlock nodded her head. "You must have been planning ways to protect your family for some time. I believe it would be wise to follow Mr Bauer's advice. Richard, William, what do you think?"

The pair looked at each other. Wordlessly, they agreed. Richard spoke for them. "We should prepare to follow Mr Bauer when we reach Bamberg."

~~ ** ~~

Elizabeth sat next to Lady Matlock, feeling drained of life. In such a short time, she had found herself without family for the first time in her life. Just a few hours ago, she was with her uncle and her beloved brother. Now Alex was dead and perhaps her uncle, too, was gone. The pain she felt was overwhelming.

The trio, with whom she was sitting, had been kind to her, caring for her needs. They had saved her from falling in the river, as Alex had pulled away from her in death. In her mind, Elizabeth wondered if it had been better if she had followed her brother to death. She felt so empty without him.

Alex had always been the one to protect her from their mother's outrage of Elizabeth's long walks in nature and her love of climbing trees. Every time she came home with her gowns dirty or torn, or her boots scuffed, Mrs Bennet would rail against her second born daughter.

"Lizzy, why can you not be like Jane? She is so sweet natured, never doing anything to make me fret. Why do you not practice on the pianoforte or paint screens? It would be less taxing on my nerves."

"Please, Mamma, do not scold Lizzy." Alex *would say. "I provoked her to climb the tree. She only climbed the tree due to my saying that no girl could reach the higher apples. If not for my words, Lizzy would never have been in the tree."*

"You are too good to your sister, Alex. You always

DARCY'S CONTINENTAL ESCAPE

take upon yourself any troubles in which she finds herself."

"Lizzy is a good girl, Mamma. She is intelligent, and loves the outdoors, much like myself. How can I not love her and wish to protect her?"

As usual, Mrs Bennet placed a kiss on her son's cheek and walked away from her least favorite daughter.

Elizabeth took hold of her brother's hand and squeezed it tightly. "My greatest thanks, Alex. What would I ever do without you?"

"You shall never know, as I will watch over you forever." Alex said, as he placed a kiss on top of her chocolate colored curls. "Now, shall we take our apples to Cook, so they will not go to waste?"

The memory of the last time Alex had covered for her misdeeds brought a fresh wave of tears to Elizabeth's eyes. How could she return to Longbourn without her dear brother? What would happen to their family, with her brother no longer the heir? All of her life, Elizabeth remembered her mother's ravings of breaking the entail on the estate, which would allow her to remain at Longbourn all of her life. With Alex gone, who would inherit the estate? Her sisters would never be able, as the entail specifically stated that only males could be the heir. But there was no other male to become the heir. Only a distant cousin who was unknown to the Bennets.

Elizabeth could not face the loss of her brother. She loved and respected him. When he was at the university, he wrote to her every week. Every Friday, she looked forward to receiving her letter, reading of his studies and his friends. Most weeks, the letters made her laugh at the hijinks in which the young men had participated. The pranks they had played on each other, and some they had played on their instructors, all made Elizabeth smile and made her feel as if she were with her brother. It had always bothered her that Alex could go to school, but she and Jane could not attend the schools with him. As Elizabeth grew older, it had always been a thorn in her side.

And now, at her darkest hour, she was alone with her memories. She no longer had a brother. She was far from her home, with no one but strangers to comfort her. How she wished she had been the one to die, or have died with Alex. All she could do was sit on the ship and pray that God would be merciful and allow her to join her brother.

~~ ** ~~

Darcy and Richard continued to go over the maps, and Bauer joined them when he could. It was clear the man knew the area.

The tension of the passengers on the ship was high. The captain came around to the passengers, asking if anyone was injured or ill, attempting to calm everyone. Darcy asked to speak with the captain.

"Sir, do you believe we are still in danger?"

"The madman who leads the French will not stop until he rules the world. We are heading west, closer to France. This river has been desired by Napoleon for some time, so it would be foolish to believe he would not have ships coming up from the Rhine to take the Danube."

"So it is best that we disembark as soon as possible? Should we go ashore at Melk or Linz?" Richard inquired.

"You could, though they are not as large as Nuremberg or Bamberg. In either of those cities, you would find the assistance you will need to find your way off the continent. And, if you go by Linz or Melk, you will need to go over the alps. It is not an easy journey."

Darcy nodded. "So we should be safe enough to make our way to Bamberg?"

"I believe you should be. But it is war, so who can be certain of anything." The captain looked at Elizabeth, huddled beside Lady Matlock. "Is she well?"

"She witnessed the young man behind her killed." Lady Matlock replied. "She is frightened."

"Forgive me. It is difficult for young ladies to see the hardships of war. It is fortunate that she was not killed. I have some extra rugs in my quarters, I will send one to you to keep her warm." The captain then moved away from the group.

Darcy looked at Elizabeth, concerned with her well-being. "Elizabeth, would you like some water?"

Elizabeth did not respond. Her eyes were staring off at nothing. Lady Matlock pulled the young lady into her embrace.

"All will be well, Elizabeth. Wait and see. All will be well. Can you tell me about your family? Besides your brother, are there other siblings?"

Elizabeth continued staring off in the distance, not seeing anything.

Darcy knelt before Elizabeth. He took hold of her hands, feeling how cold they were, and began chaffing them to bring warmth back in her fingers. "Elizabeth, would you mind telling us about yourself? How old are you? Do you enjoy reading or music? We will be together for some time, it would be nice to know your likes and dislikes."

One of the men who worked upon the ship moved towards the group, carrying a rug in his hands. "The captain said the miss could use this to keep warm. You folk be needing anything else?"

The men shook their heads, but Lady Matlock spoke. "Is there a chance of getting something for Elizabeth to eat? Even a simple biscuit may bring her some comfort."

"Let me see what I can find. We did not get our supplies in Vienna, as there was no time. We will gather supplies further up the way."

"Anything you can find would be appreciated." Richard responded. "Do you know how long it will be until we arrive at Bamberg?"

"Several hours. You might as well sit and rest. We will let you know when we are near."

Standing up, Darcy unfolded the rug and wrapped it around Elizabeth's shoulders, tucking it tightly in front of her. "You are safe, Elizabeth. Have no fear. We will protect you."

Lady Matlock again pulled Elizabeth to her. The pair of ladies rocked back and forth, as Lady Matlock hummed a lullaby.

Taking the advice of the man who brought the rug to them, Darcy took his seat next to his aunt and the young lady who had become part of their party. There was something about the young lady that drew him to her. He could not be certain what was making him wish to pull her into his embrace, but he felt extremely protective towards her.

A dream came to him as he slept. A pleasant dream, of a day at home, on his family's estate of Pemberley. It was one of the largest estates in Derbyshire, if not in England. Darcy was most comfortable when he was at the estate, where he could be one with the land. He had never been comfortable in society, especially if there were a large group of people. It was known that he was heir to one of the wealthiest families, and brought out those who wished for connections due to fortune or a place in the highest circles of society.

Fitzwilliam Darcy had always been shy, unable to find his tongue when in large parties. The newest trend of clothing or gaming did not interest him. He did not partake of the seedier pursuits that others of his station enjoyed. No, his family and his estate were the most important aspects in his life.

In his dream, he was riding his favorite stallion, Apollo. The horse had been given to him for his last birthday. The only sad part of his last birthday was that his mother was no longer with them to celebrate. Nearly a year had passed since Lady Anne Darcy, nee Fitzwilliam, had died during childbirth. The child joined his mother in death. Gerald Darcy had been devastated, as he dearly loved his wife and family.

The dream had Darcy riding across an area of Pemberley which lead to a small pond. Near the pond was a copse of trees, and a delightful area where his family often shared picnics. As his horse approached the area, he could see a young lady with beautiful chocolate colored locks, unpinned, flowing curls down her back and over her shoulders. She was lying on a rug on the earth, propped on her elbows, as she was reading a book. Hearing his horse approaching, the young lady turned and waved to him. The sparkle in her eyes was amazing. It warmed his heart to see her, and he waved back to her, hurrying to be at her side.

As he knelt on the ground beside her, Darcy reached over to place a kiss on her lips, when suddenly he could hear his aunt's voice.

"William, we should prepare to disembark. We are at Bamberg."

Darcy's eyes opened, surprising him that he was not at Pemberley. It had seemed so real. But how could it be real. He had only met the young lady who invaded his dream, and she had never been at

Pemberley.

"Yes...Yes, I will gather my belongings." Darcy stood quickly.

Lady Matlock shook her head, a smile gracing her lips. It was clear that the young lady she held in an embrace was having an effect on her nephew. She prayed that all would be well. Elizabeth had already lost her brother, and they were all still in danger.

~~~~~~~ ** ~~~~~~~

Chapter 3

The ship came to a stop at the docks, and everyone began disembarking. Darcy and Richard took care of the luggage they and the ladies had brought, and followed Bauer from the ship, while Lady Matlock escorted Elizabeth. The young lady was still in a state of shock, barely responding to anything said or done around her. Lady Matlock hoped that she would soon be able to recover.

Bauer led the group to the Abbey, taking them to a small building behind the relic of the Abbey. The small building turned out to be a place for the grounds keeper to reside. Inside, they found an older man, who was named Mr Hoffman. He was a cousin to Bauer.

"What are you doing here?" Hoffman asked. "Who are these people?"

"Vienna is under attack. These people fled on the ship to escape. I have offered to assist them to return to England."

Hoffman looked at his cousin. "So you plan to leave your homeland? You intend to journey to this foreign land?"

"It is my wife's home. It will be safer for her and our children to be away from here. What would happen if Napoleon's army finds her here? She will be killed, most likely my children as well. I will not remain here, putting them in the path of danger. We must make the journey now."

Mr Hoffman nodded his head. "Your Emily is a good woman. I would not like to see her harmed. If the French have taken the Danube, it will not be long before they are here. What can I do to assist you?"

"Can they remain here, while I go to my house, to speak with Emily? When I return, I will stay here, with them, while you make purchases for us. Their clothes will show that they are wealthy. I wish to keep them protected, so we will need to purchase clothing suitable for those of a lower class, perhaps of those in trade. We will need to have supplies, food and blankets. They have the funds to purchase all we require."

Mr Hoffman nodded his head again. "Go swiftly, and bring your wife and children here. Then I will make the necessary purchases. While you are gone, we will make a list of what will be needed. Will your wagon be able to make such a journey?"

"It should be fine. We will make our way, by land, to Cologne. From there, we will find a ship heading north on the Rhine." Bauer stated. "So we should have no problems reaching there with my wagon."

"Then off with you. I will keep the English here."

Bauer introduced Lady Matlock and the three younger people to Hoffman. The older man bowed. "Though I wish it had been under better circumstances, I welcome you to Michaelsberg Abbey. It is no longer an abbey, as it is now a refuge for the elderly and the ill."

"Mr Hoffman, we cannot thank you enough for your kindness." Lady Matlock curtsied to the man. "I will see that you are properly compensated for all that you do for us."

"That is not necessary, Madame. I trust that God has shown you here, and it is my duty to God to be of service to you. Now, would you care for some refreshments? I have some tea, some cold meat and bread."

As if in response, Darcy's stomach growled loudly, causing the group to laugh. Mr Hoffman smiled. "I will accept that as a response in favor. Come, we will go to the kitchens."

Mr Hoffman led them through the buildings, until they reached the kitchen. The cook was preparing the evening meal for those who lived at the Abbey, and was willing to share with the newcomers, especially when Darcy placed some coins on the table. As they ate, Mr Hoffman spoke.

"Have you ever visited Bamberg? You are from England, if I am correct."

Lady Matlock nodded her head. "My family is from Vienna, but my husband and his family are from England. We have been visiting my sister, in Vienna, when we received word of the French invading."

"Napoleon will never stop invading, not until he rules the world." Mr Hoffman said, his expression was as if he had tasted something extremely foul. "Have you heard of our Abbey before today?"

"I have heard of the Abbey, though I have never seen it before today." Lady Matlock answered. "My children have never been to the continent before this journey."

"Not the way to take a holiday. I would prefer to remain here, safe from the world. The Abbey has been here for hundreds of years, and withstood much. The original building was built around 1015. Since then, it has been plundered by townspeople in the 1400's, and again in the 1500's. There have been earthquakes and fires. But the Abbey is still here. It was originally a Benedictine monastery. If you wish, while we wait for Bauer to return, I would be willing

DARCY'S CONTINENTAL ESCAPE

to show you around the buildings and gardens."

"You are kind, Mr Hoffman. It would be pleasant to see the Abbey." Lady Matlock declared.

The group ate the bread and cheese they had been given, along with some soup. Once they had finished, they began the tour. As they walked through the buildings and the gardens, their guide informed them of their surroundings. Mr Hoffman was a devoted grounds keeper, and he knew much of the history of the Abbey and Bamberg.

"I have lived here all of my life. My father was grounds keeper before me, as was his father before him. The Hoffman family has seen to the gardens here for generations. Each bloom of a flower and every blade of grass has been tended by a member of my family."

"The Holy Roman Emperor Henry II established the bishopric here in Bamberg. If you noticed, when you arrived in Bamberg, each of the seven hills has a church at the top. This hill was known as Michaelsberg, or Mount St. Michaels. Emperor Henry and his wife, Cunigunde, are buried in our cemetery."

"The author, Prior Frutolf of Michelsberg lived here until his death, in 1103. The Abbey then came under the rule of Bishop Otto, who was later buried here. He was later canonized, which gave the Abbey papal protection. The Abbey owned much of the lands in this area. In 1435, there was a conflict with the townspeople, resulting in their plundering the grounds for whatever they could steal. The Peasant war of 1525 resulted in more suffering, as the Abbey was occupied by forces. In the 1600's, Bamberg saw a dark time, when it is believed around one thousand people lost their lives during the witch trials. From 1626 to 1631, under the rule of Prince-Bishop Johann Georg II Fuchs von Dornheim. The infamous witch prison, Drudenhaus, was built in 1627 in Bamberg."

"In 1647, the Academia Bambergensis was founded, bringing education to the area. In 1759, there were changes in the diocese, and Bamberg lost lands and independence by 1803, with the secularization of the church lands, making Bamberg part of Bavaria. The Abbey buildings and possessions transferred to the city, and the monks were forced to leave the monastery. That is when the Abbey was transferred into the almshouses."

As they entered the nave, Mr Hoffman continued. "Due to a fire in 1610, the nave and the westwork, including two west towers, were rebuilt from scratch. If you look at the ceiling, the paintings are referred to as the Garden of Heaven, with five hundred and seventy-eight different flowers and herbs displayed there. The Garden of Heaven was finished in 1617."

The ceiling was elegantly done, impressing the visitors. Lady Matlock was grateful for the information the elder man had provided. "Mr Hoffman, it is a sign of your devotion to the Abbey, your being able to share the history of this grand place. I am grateful for your giving us the tour. In this time of trouble, to see such history is a blessing. Would you mind if we were to say a prayer for a safe journey to come?"

"By all means, please take your time. Would you prefer me to step outside, allowing you some privacy?"

Lady Matlock shook her head. "No, there is no need for you to leave. You have family who will be with us, so the prayer includes them."

"You will see to their protection?" The man was hesitant. It was unusual for the wealthy to care for those who were beneath them.

Darcy stepped forward. "You have my promise to protect them as we protect our own family. It is a shared journey we are making, not a sightseeing excursion. Without Mr Bauer and his wife, we would be in more danger. And we will see them protected when we arrive in England."

"You are far different than the wealthy I have known." Mr Hoffman stated. "And I am grateful that my family has found you. They deserve a good future. Their children deserve a future."

"And they will have the best we can give them."

"While you are here, I will make my way to the mercantile. I will purchase clothes and supplies. Is there anything else you will require?" Hoffman inquired.

"Whatever we will need for the journey. Clothing for each of us, so we will blend in with the everyone, food supplies, and we will require water." Lady Matlock stated, motioning to her nephew to give the man the funds he would require.

"Please remain inside while I am away. I wish for your presence to be kept from as many people as possible."

~~ ** ~~

The family kept to the church, discussing the journey before them. Elizabeth still remained quiet, though she had been able to feed herself when prompted by Lady Matlock. Mr Hoffman was gone for close to an hour when he returned. "We can use the rooms down the hall, so you can change into these clothes. Forgive me, I know they are quite plain, but it will be safer for all of you."

Lady Matlock and Elizabeth entered the first room to which Hoffman led them to, while Richard and Darcy took the second one, across the hall from the first. Lady Matlock was able to assist Elizabeth into the plain muslin gown. Once both of the ladies were dressed, Lady Matlock fashioned their hair in a plain and simple fashion.

"There, my dear girl. I believe we will blend in with the residents here. We will have to be careful, not letting on that we are wealthy. And we will have to take on tasks that most in our society would never dare. Are you up to the challenge?"

When Elizabeth did not look up or respond, Lady Matlock stood in front of her. Taking her hand, she carefully lifted Elizabeth's chin until the young lady looked in her eyes.

"Elizabeth, I know you are mourning your loss. Believe me, I understand your pain. But your brother would not approve of your behavior. I am certain that he would wish for you to do all that you can to survive, to return to England, and to the rest of your family. We need you to do your part, to protect us all from what this journey will hold for us. It will be dangerous, and we will need to use all of our courage and intelligence to ensure our survival. If we are captured by the French forces, we could be killed, or we can be violated in the worst way a woman could.

Please tell me you understand. Please, speak with me, so I can be certain of your understanding."

A spark of life began to glow in the pair of fine eyes that had, a moment before, been empty and lifeless. Elizabeth was able to respond. "Y...yes, Lady Matlock."

"No, for all of our protection, you cannot call me by my title. Please remember. We will all be in danger if someone learns I am a Countess. We are traveling as a family, and you must remember that I am Mamma. Richard and William are your brothers, for this journey. Please, you must remember."

"I will...M...Mamma." Elizabeth stated, her voice was shaky.

Lady Matlock pulled the young lady into her embrace. "When I was a young lady, near your age, my brother was killed in a carriage accident. He was my twin brother, and we had been very close. It was devastating, so I understand how you must be feeling. My brother was a sweet boy, always watching over me. I was not very ladylike in my younger days. And my mother was constantly complaining for me to behave properly. Matthew was my protector."

"Adam did the same for me." Elizabeth said, tears flowing down her cheeks. "He was the best brother."

"And he would wish for you to survive, would he not?"

Elizabeth nodded her head. "He would. Our parents, they will be devastated. He is...was the heir. Adam's birth broke the entail on our father's estate. Our father was planning to turn over the running of the estate to Adam, after Adam and I returned from this trip."

"And you were visiting family?"

"Our uncle. My mother's brother. He has lived in Vienna for many years. Uncle refused to leave Vienna, as he lives in the house he shared with his beloved wife. She died years ago, though he feels close to her in their home."

"A love match...those should be treasured. My own marriage was one of convenience, a business deal to bring financial support to my husband. He is the Earl of Matlock. His father was a gambler, and he wasted most of the income from the estate. My dowry was used to stabilize the estate, assist in making the repairs that were desperately needed to keep the estate from having to be sold."

"Do you...do you care for your husband?"

Lady Matlock smiled. "We are friends, nothing more. But that is far better than many a marriage of our circle of society can claim."

"I cannot thank you, for all you are doing for me. My brother...he had our funds in his coat pocket. When we arrive in England, I will speak with my father..."

"There is no need to worry, dear girl. We have enough to see all of us to safety. Before we left my sister's home, she saw that we had all of the funds she had at her house, and with the funds we had brought with us, we will be fine. We will not be traveling in the lap of luxury, but we will make the journey. That is what is most important."

"I can do a little cooking, if need be. Nothing fancy, but I can make sure that we do not starve." Elizabeth's expression was pleading, as she looked up at Lady Matlock.

"We will all do our share of the work that is before us." Lady Matlock placed a kiss on Elizabeth's forehead. "We will all do our share."

~~ ** ~~

Mr Bauer arrived as the sun was beginning to set. In his wagon were his wife and children. He quickly made his way inside the building. "We must leave, immediately."

"What is wrong?" Richard asked.

"French army have arrived in Bamberg. They are at the edge of the city, and the battle is beginning. We need to leave as soon as possible."

Everyone looked at each other, fear taking hold of them. Finally, Richard spoke. "Mother, we must go. If we remain here, we could be taken prisoners, or killed."

"Yes, of course. Elizabeth, you and William go on to the wagon. Richard, take the two bags we packed to take with us." Lady Matlock commanded the younger members of her group. She then turned her attention to Mr Hoffman. "Sir, you will be in danger if you remain here. Are you sure you do not wish to join us?"

"It is my home. Though I appreciate your offer, I must protect the Abbey and its occupants to the best of my abilities. But you must make haste. My cousin is a good man; he will do all he can to protect your family."

"If you ever find yourself in England, please contact us. We will always welcome you, for all the kindness you have shared with us."

"My thanks, madam. Now, off with you."

Lady Matlock made her way to the waiting wagon. It was a large wagon, mostly used for hauling freight for the mercantile. Mr Bauer had purchased it before going to his home. On the wagon was a young lady, near the same age as her son. She was holding an infant in her arms, with another child, who appeared to be around three years old, sitting beside her. Mr Bauer introduced his wife, Emily, to Lady Matlock.

"Please, call me Klarissa. As we are making this journey together, we had best be as informal as possible. You have met my son, Richard. William is my nephew, though for the journey, he will refer to me as his mother. Miss Elizabeth is a gentlewoman from England, who has been separated from her loved ones after a tragedy. She will be referring to me as her mother as well. Perhaps it will be best to pose as related, so you may refer to me as Aunt Klarissa."

"But it is not proper, your ladyship." Emily Bauer stated.

"With the French approaching and our lives in jeopardy, there is no need for proper etiquette. If anyone were to discover who we are, we could be taken hostage, to be ransomed, or killed outright for what funds we have with us. It would also endanger your family. So please, my name is Aunt Klarissa. And Richard, William, and Elizabeth are my children."

Emily looked at her husband. "V...very well. And I am Emily. Our children are Brigit, who is turning three next month, and Gretchen, who is two months old. And my husband is Dietrich. Or Trich, as I refer to him."

Lady Matlock smiled. "Well, I suggest we make haste. We do not wish to meet with the invaders."

~~~~~~~ ** ~~~~~~~

Chapter 4

The wagon was hampered by many people attempting to escape the oncoming threat of battle. Many people were in the streets, as they made their way out of the city. Most of the people were on foot, though there were a few wagons and carriages attempting to flee. Those on foot begged and pleaded with those with carriages and wagons, holding out small children to be taken to safety or asking for an elderly loved one to be conveyed.

Explosions could be heard in the distance, making everyone nervous. The horses were skittish, not being able to run with the crowds of people flocking the streets. Trich had to concentrate on the team, while Richard kept watch over the people who attempted to climb on board their wagon. Darcy was near the back of the wagon, attempting to protect the women from being pulled out to make room for those unfortunate to be on foot. Screams and wails were heard, as people were being trampled by the crowd.

As the battle sounds intensified, those on foot became frantic. They were desperate to escape the army approaching, and desperation can lead the best of men to behave badly.

The wagon approached the bridge which they would cross over the Regnitz River. Hordes of people were pushing their way to gain access to the bridge, with some of the people falling in the river. One man grabbed hold of Darcy's arm, pulling him in an attempt to dislodge him from his place on the wagon.

"Let me on, I need your wagon for my family."

"Release me. You will not take our wagon." Darcy replied, beating on the man with his free hand, desperate to remain in the wagon. Seeing what was happening, Elizabeth reached over in hopes to free Darcy from the man's grasp. When she was unsuccessful, she sat in a position which allowed her free use of her legs. She began kicking the man in the face, stunning him to a point that he let go of Darcy. The man stumbled about, blood flowing from his obviously broken nose. The last sight they had of the man was as he was pushed out of the way of the rest of the pedestrians. After witnessing the failed attempt to take the wagon by force, and the fact that Darcy pulled out his pistol, no one else was prepared to challenge the group.

Lady Matlock had reached into her satchel and removed two knives. She handed one to Elizabeth, keeping the other for herself. "Elizabeth, keep this ready. If anyone else makes even the slightest move towards taking our wagon, use the knife."

Her words were loud and clear. The grand woman knew how to make her point in a manner that brooked no argument. She looked at Richard, who had turned when he heard his mother's voice. His pride in the woman who had birthed him was tremendous. Unlike many ladies of the upper circles of society, Klarissa Fitzwilliam was no wilting flower. She was a sturdy oak tree, standing tall and proud, and taking on whatever challenges life threw her way.

Giving her son an arched eyebrow look, he held out his hand to show her that he was armed with a large bladed knife, one he usually carried strapped to his leg. She knew he aspired to join the army in England, and he had studied methods to defend himself while at the university. Klarissa looked at Emily and the children.

"Brigit, dear one, come to Auntie Klarissa. Let me hold you, little one."

The little girl looked cautiously to her mother, and seeing her mother's approval, Brigit moved to Klarissa's embrace. With the affection of a mother, Klarissa wiped the tears from the child's cheeks, then began to hum to her. With the world around them in chaos, Klarissa was able to shelter the child from the violence and fear.

Finally, the wagon was on the bridge, though

moving slowly. Suddenly, a young lady thrust a wrapped bundle into the bed of the wagon, then disappeared into the crowd. Darcy was shocked, though he continued scanning the crowd for the young lady. Elizabeth picked up the bundle and began to unwrap, shocked when the bundle was a small child.

"Where did she go?" Elizabeth looked up. "Where is the mother? Why would she throw her infant into our wagon and disappear?"

Klarissa looked at the baby, and was surprised to find the child was still asleep, considering all that was happening around them. "I do not know, Elizabeth, though she may have felt it was safer for the babe to be with us. William, did you get a good look at the mother?"

Darcy shook his head. "There were too many people surrounding the wagon. It was difficult to see who thrust the child into the wagon. Was it injured?"

"I do not see any marks or wounds." Klarissa replied. "Hopefully the child is well."

"What are we to do with someone's infant?" Darcy asked, the look on his face was of surprise. Other than his younger sister, he had rarely been around babies, and was uncomfortable with them.

"We will have to take the child with us, until we discover who are its parents. The parents must be terrified, to thrust their infant into the arms of complete strangers."

Elizabeth was holding the child to her chest. "What will happen if we never find the mother? What will become of the little one?"

"We will cross that bridge when we get there." Klarissa said. "For the moment, let us concentrate on safely leaving Bamberg."

The chaos continued to run freely through the mob of people fleeing the city and the incoming forces. The closer the sounds of battle came, the greater fear ruled the citizens of Bamberg. Darcy continued watching the crowd, ensuring that no one was able to overtake their wagon. The day seemed endless, and time appeared to be frozen for those who were attempting to escape the threat of the French Invasion.

After what seemed to be hours, the wagon and its occupants were reaching the northern boundaries of Bamberg. People were still rushing, but as they reached an open area, with no buildings or confined bridges, the people were able to scatter easier.

"We can finally push the team to speed up their step." Richard said.

Elizabeth began to panic. "But the child. What will happen with the child?"

Emily looked at her new friend. "Most likely the babe would have been killed by the invaders. If I had no other option to protect my children, I would likely have done the same."

"We are taking the child with us?"

"If we leave the child here, we are possibly leaving it to be murdered by the coming army. Would you leave a child behind, knowing that might end with the child's death?"

Looking to the sweet face of the cherub in her arms, Elizabeth shook her head. "I could never do anything that would cause the death of anyone, especially not a child."

Darcy looked at the child. "Is it a boy or girl?"

Elizabeth pulled back the cloth that was wrapped around the child's bottom. "It is a boy."

"I would say he is near six months of age. Since he will be with us for the unforeseen future, we should choose a name for which to call him." Klarissa determined.

Several names were offered by Richard, Emily, and Klarissa, but it was Darcy who finally declared a name that Elizabeth agreed with. "He looks like a Thomas." Darcy had said.

A smile graced Elizabeth's lips. "That is my father's name, and my brother's middle name. I believe the name Thomas Alexander fits this young man. Thomas Alexander."

The group all agreed with the choice. Emily was surprised that Thomas had yet to wake. "Are you certain he is breathing properly?" The young mother was concerned.

Klarissa held her finger to the boy's lips, and there was a slight movement, as the natural tendency of an infant who nursed. "He is alive. I am not certain, but I wonder if the mother gave him something to aid the babe to sleep. Perhaps to make it simpler for her as they fled from the invasion."

"If the mother had needed to hide, a slumbering infant would be easier with which to hide." Richard stated.

Trich pointed towards an area to the west of them. "I suggest we stop up ahead, at the farm of a friend of mine. Joseph is a good man, he will give us some food for the horses and some water. We need to reserve the supplies we have, as we are not sure what will be available, the further we journey from Bamberg."

Richard nodded his head. "Indeed, that is a sound suggestion. And most of the people are scurrying towards the east, so we should be safer."

Another hour went by before the wagon came to a halt outside a small farm house.

A man's voice came from inside the house. "Who are you? What are you doing here?"

"Joseph, it is me, Trich. We need some water and feed for the horses."

"What are you doing here? Why are you out on a night like this? It is too dangerous. You should be in your home."

"We are leaving. I have my family with me."

The man came out of his front door, holding a rifle. "You are wise. If only I could join you."

Richard looked at the man. "You are welcome to join us. We would need another wagon, but you are welcome."

Joseph frowned slightly. "You are English?"

Trich nodded his head. "Cousins of Emily's. They were visiting, when the French attacked Bamberg. I need to take them to Cologne, to the ships north."

"If you need to tend your horses, do so quickly.

Then you need to be off. I cannot afford to be caught with English at my home." Joseph was concerned.

"If we can rest here for an hour, we would be grateful." Emily said. "My little ones need to be fed, and my aunt needs to rest from the road. It was terrible in the city, very dangerous. We had to fight to keep the wagon and horses."

"Then feed your children and tend your horses. As I said, I do not wish to be caught with English at my home."

Emily and the children were escorted into the house, towards the fireplace, where a blaze was glowing. An elderly woman was sitting in a rocking chair near the hearth.

"Emily…why are you here this time of night?"

"French have attacked the city. We needed to escape." The young lady replied. "This is my cousin, Elizabeth, and my aunt, Klarissa. They were visiting us, from England, with my other cousins."

"It is dangerous to be here, especially for English. They will be murdered. And you, you are English girl. You must not stay here."

Emily shook her head. "We are leaving the area. It was a difficult time getting this far from the city, so we stopped to give the horses a rest and allow me to see to the children."

"The little ones, oh, the dear little ones. You need to keep them safe."

"We will, Helga. Have no fear. We have inherited an extra child."

Helga frowned. She was in her sixties, and had lived at the farm all of her life. She had grown up with her father farming the land, then her husband came to aid her aging father. When her father had died, and Helga had given birth to her son, Joseph, he grew up caring for the family farm. Unfortunately, Joseph and Helga were the only ones left of their family. She loved children, and was considered the grandmother for all the children of the neighborhood. Emily motioned for Elizabeth to carry Thomas to the elder woman, hoping that Helga might know of the child's family.

"I have never seen this child. Where did you find him?"

"When we were at the bridge, attempting to flee the city, people were surrounding us. We had a difficult time keeping them from knocking us from the wagon, as many wished the wagon and horses to escape. Someone threw this child onto the wagon, but we could not find the person. We believe the person was the mother."

Tears welled in the elder lady's eyes. "I am not surprised, though it tears my heart. A desperate mother would do anything to protect her child."

"So you have not seen him before?" Klarissa asked.

"No, not this child. Will you take him with you?"

Emily looked at the child, still nestled in Elizabeth's arms. "If we cannot find anyone to take him, we must take him with us. Do you know of anyone?"

Helga shook her head. "No…no…but you will need clothes and such for him. I have some I have been making for the children of the neighborhood." She stepped to a door leading to a bedchamber. The ladies heard sounds of things being moved about in the room, and then Helga returned, a broad smile on her lips. She held out a pile of clothes. "Take these…take them. The little one will need them. And this cover…keep him warm."

Emily was shown to the bedchambers, with her infant and little Thomas. The other ladies stayed in the main room, as the young mother nursed Gretchen and Thomas. Elizabeth saw to Brigit having a bit of bread and cheese, while Klarissa and Helga chatted.

"If you and your son wish to come with us, you are welcome. We would be a tight fit, but we can make room for you on the wagon." Klarissa stated.

The elderly woman shook her head. "My dear girl, I have never lived anywhere but here. I could not leave this farm, it is my family, my roots. No, if it is my time to join my dear Wilbur, I will do so with no regrets. But you are English, you need to leave the area. It will not be safe, not now."

Once the children were fed, the horses watered and rested, the wagon was loaded once again, and the ragtag group was off again. Before they left, Trich gave his friend the key to his home. "If there is anything you want you are welcome to take it. We will not be coming back."

Joseph nodded his head. "We will keep you in our prayers. Be safe."

~~~~~~~ ** ~~~~~~~

Chapter 5

Elizabeth fell asleep, leaning against Darcy's shoulder, with Thomas on her lap. Though the child had been awake for short periods, they were all certain that the boy had likely been given some spirits to keep him calm. He spent most of the night sleeping, waking only once.

Darcy was exhausted, but he remained awake, watching over the passengers of the wagon. Richard had moved to the wagon bed, dozing off for a while, as he would take over driving when Trich was ready to sleep. The men were adamant that they should only stop for short periods, and keep moving, through the night and most of the following day. Each man would take a turn driving, allowing them to put as much distance between them and the invading army.

Klarissa smiled at the vision of her nephew, with Elizabeth and Thomas at his side. She could not wait for her boys, including her nephew, to find wives and have children. If there was one thing that Klarissa made clear to the men in her life, it was that she wished for grandchildren. As Darcy's mother had died many years before, Klarissa had declared it her duty to act as grandmother for Darcy's children.

Darcy looked up, noticing his aunt's expression. "What are you smiling at, Aunt?"

"You, my dear William. I am thinking of how I look forward to seeing you married and a father. I plan on spoiling your children, just as I will my grandchildren."

His eyes rolled, as he had heard his aunt's constant badgering of her sons when it came to their settling down. "We have the French army attacking, and we are fleeing for our lives, and you are dreaming of the day I am married and a father. Aunt Klarissa, you astound me."

"I am a mother, what do you expect from me? I need children to indulge and love. When you are facing the worst times in your life, you must concentrate on the good things to come. And grandchildren will be the best things to come to my life. So you remember, as soon as we are safe and returned to England, I will not rest until you are married and children are on their way.

Darcy chuckled. "You are relentless, Aunt. We have nothing to fear from the French, you are determined enough to keep them away from us just because it is your wish. A wall will spring up from the ground to block the army from finding us."

"Well, I was going to keep that a secret until it was absolutely necessary for you to know. I am quite powerful, you know." Klarissa gave a smile, reminding her nephew of the term, a cat that ate the canary.

The wagon rolled on, passing through the town of Schweinfurt. The area had suffered considerable damage over the past years, as Napoleon's army attempted to control the area. The damage was clear to see, as was the poverty of those who lived there.

Emily shared some of the history of the town, speaking of a friend who had died when the fighting had last been in the area. "Marcus and his family owned a confectionary shop. He was defending his shop from the invaders, who were stealing everything he owned. His wife, Margrit, survived, though they had beaten her…violating her. She told me that she wished she had died with her husband."

"It amazes me the way men behave during war." Klarissa stated. "Were these men the sort who would violate a woman, before the war? Did the battle make the men feel free to commit such acts? What if it were their women, how would they feel about someone committing such acts on them?"

Darcy shook his head. "One of our professors at the university discussed such phenomenon. How a man of honor can be caught up in the whirlwind of behavior during war time, behaving in a manner he would never have done before. He questioned many soldiers who had been in battle, and used their answers in his research."

"Professor Monteford?" Richard asked.

"Yes. It was interesting, some of the men were horribly ashamed of their behavior, surprised that they had participated in such atrocities. Professor Monteford told of one man, who had been married and a father, had participated in beating a man to death, after raping his wife and daughter. The soldier felt so guilty after the event, and after years of being home, with his own family, he took his life. He could no longer live with what he had done."

Elizabeth spoke. "My father had been on holiday from the university, when he learned of some classmates who had gone on a drunk. The group terrorized several of the local businesses, and took advantage of several young ladies. One of my father's dearest friends was in the group, and, after he sobered, he was appalled at his own behavior. He fled England, and is living in Canada. The man never married, as he told my father that he felt he did not deserve to be loved."

"Where did your father attend?" Darcy asked.

"Oxford. He considered it a bit of heaven, as he

has a great fondness for books. Papa has always teased that if he had a library as large as the university, he would never leave the room." A small smile crept out of Elizabeth. "My brother just graduated from Oxford."

"You were visiting a relative in Vienna?"

"My mother's elder brother. He has lived in Vienna for many years, and Papa felt it would be like a grand tour for Alex. And my brother knew how dear the journey would be to me, so he begged Papa to allow me to join him."

Klarissa joined in the conversation. "Did your father not wish to make the journey? Why did neither of your parents join you?"

"Papa does not like to be away from home, and especially his book room. Mamma would have come, but she was needed to be home with my sisters. My elder sister, Jane, was being courted by a young man who is visiting our neighborhood. Jane does not believe anything will come of the situation, but Mamma is firm in her belief that the young man will propose. He wrote some very...sad...poems. Mamma felt that it was declaring himself and his desire to marry my sister. Personally, I believe that one poor sonnet can drive love away."

This caused Darcy to chuckle. "I thought poetry

was the food of love."

"If it is a strong, devoted sort, it may feed the love, though I believe that if it is a weak sort of relationship, one poor line can smother any spark completely."

This brought forth laughs from Klarissa and Darcy. The elder lady inquired about the other members of the Bennet family.

"Alex was the eldest, which was of great relief to my mother. The estate was entailed away from the female line, and Mamma has often stated that if it had not been for Alex, we would have faced living in the hedgerow if the estate had been inherited by my father's distant cousin. But Alex's birth broke the entail. After Alex is Jane. She is the perfect daughter, as my mother has been quoted many times. There is no one in the world as beautiful and as sweet as my dearest sister. Jane is truly an angel on earth."

"If she is anything as pretty as you, she must be beautiful." Klarissa said.

"Oh, no, Mamma has told me many times that I am in no way as beautiful as Jane. My sister has golden hair, crystal blue eyes, and has never said a cross word to or about anyone."

"Impossible." Darcy declared. "It is not possible to

never say a cross word. My sister is good natured, but she has even held ill thoughts of others."

"Not Jane. No matter how odious the person behaves, Jane will find something good to say about them." Elizabeth smiled. "I am next in line, followed by Mary. Mary is … well, Mary is … very studious in all things religious. She has memorized Fordyce Sermons and any theological books she can find. Papa has stated many times that it was a shame that Mary was born a female, for she would have been a perfect clergyman."

Everyone chuckled at this declaration. Richard inquired to the remaining sisters.

"The last two were twins. Katherine, who we call Kitty, and Lydia. And they are always together. Mamma says that she is surprised they were not born stuck together. They are silly girls, only fourteen years old. Their fondest joys are found dreaming of flirting with the militia that is camped in the market town of Meryton. They both have declared their desire to marry a man in a red coat. According to my sisters, they are the only men worth marrying."

"Do you have any other relations? Aunts or uncles?" Darcy inquired. He did not understand why he found himself interested in the young lady's family. There was something about Elizabeth that drew him to her.

"My father has a sister, she is a widow and lives in Ireland with her husband's sister. My mother has a sister who is married to a solicitor in Meryton and her younger brother who lives in Cheapside with his wife and their two children. Uncle Edward and Aunt Helen are very kind to us. They have welcomed Alex, Jane and me to visit them every year. Uncle owns a successful import business, Gardiner Imports. I love exploring the warehouse, to see the items that come from all over the world."

"You seem to be content with life, Elizabeth. Do you not wish to live in a grand house and be one of the grand ladies of the *ton*?" Klarissa inquired.

Elizabeth looked at Thomas, sleeping in her lap. "I would be happy with a comfortable home, a husband who loved me, and several children to keep me young. I have no need for riches."

"I am certain you will find your desire, Elizabeth. You are a rare and wonderful breath of fresh air." Darcy spoke softly.

After several moments of silence, Elizabeth determined it was time to learn more of her companions. "William, how is it that you are here with your aunt and cousin? Where are your parents or siblings?"

Klarissa listened to the conversation with a spark of hope taking light in her chest. She had already come to admire the young lady who was traveling with them.

Darcy smiled. "Aunt Klarissa was born and lived her youth in Vienna. She then married my mother's brother, Henry Fitzwilliam. They have two sons, of which Richard is the second born. My uncle's estate is Matlock, in northern Derbyshire. As for me, my mother died a little more than fourteen years ago, with the birth of my sister. My father is still living, though his health did not allow him to make such a journey. Now, with all that has happened, I am grateful Father did not come on this holiday."

"And are there other relations?" Elizabeth teased.

"Oh, you do not wish to know his other aunt." Klarissa boldly announced. "She makes Napoleon's army look mild, as she is a force with which to be reckoned."

Elizabeth's brow lifted as she took in the information. "A force with which to be reckoned? My goodness, I must learn more of this lady."

Richard snorted. "Aunt Catherine is no lady. She is one of the most obnoxious, opinionated women in all of England."

"Richard...Catherine is still your elder, show some respect." Klarissa bit her bottom lip between her teeth to keep herself from laughing. "Elizabeth, believe me, my sister in law is...unique."

"And she is adamant that I marry her only child. Aunt Catherine named her daughter after my mother, and has told me for years that it was my mother's greatest desire that Anne and I wed." Darcy shook his head as he spoke. "It was one of the reasons I was anxious to come on this holiday. If I had not, Father said I would have to join him in visiting Aunt Catherine and Anne."

"And I thought you wished to be with us because you were devastated to be separated from me." Richard laughed.

Klarissa smiled. "As you can likely surmise, Elizabeth, Richard and William have always been the best of friends. They are more brothers than cousins."

A bit of melancholy swept over Elizabeth's expression. "My family will be devastated when they learn of Alex's death. Especially Mamma, as she has always doted on him. She will likely be furious with me."

"Why would she be furious with you?" Darcy asked. He could not keep a frown from developing.

"It is my fault that Alex was killed. He was behind me, protecting me, when he was shot. And I was unable to keep him from falling in the river, so I cannot even take his body home to be buried in the family plot. Mamma will place the blame on me, as she knows that my brother would do anything he could to protect me."

This caused Darcy to become protective of the young lady beside him. "How could anyone blame you for what happened? Especially a mother, who should be grateful for your survival. She could have lost two children rather than one."

"I have never been a favorite of my mother's." Elizabeth felt tears beginning to sting her eyes. "I am my father's favorite, and Mamma does not approve of my behavior. She constantly informs me that young ladies will not attract a husband if she is constantly reading books that are meant for men. And men do not appreciate an impertinent young lady who is not demure and ladylike at all times."

Darcy's arm wrapped around Elizabeth's shoulders, pulling her closer to his body. "Your mother is a fool, if she does not approve of you. In the short time I have known you, I have found you to be all that a young lady should be, especially given the situation in which we find ourselves. How many young ladies of the *ton* would have been able to keep their wits about them while attempting to escape a war?"

The warmth and comfort Elizabeth was deriving from the actions and words from Darcy outweighed the improper nature of his embrace. Lady Matlock could see that her nephew was taken by this young lady, for she was unusual from other young ladies. Rather than simpering and agreeing with everything that Darcy said, Elizabeth spoke her mind. She gave no pretense, she did not agree with what was said simply to garner someone's good opinion.

~~ ** ~~

The group had traveled throughout the night, taking small breaks to keep from overworking the horses. Finally, they came to the city of Fulda. Near the edge of the city, they came across a stable. Trich stated he would check with the owner, to see if they could exchange the horses, or, at the least, if they could rest in the stable for a few hours.

Everyone held their breath as Trich went inside the stable, speaking with the owner. When he came back to the wagon, he looked around, as if he were making sure no one was watching.

"The owner is willing to allow us to rest in the hayloft. He said that there have been soldiers through the area for several days, but there are not any now.

We can rest a few hours, as he has no horses to spare. The soldiers took all he had, and if they return, they will likely take ours. It would be best if Richard and I rested, if you would keep a watch, William."

It was agreed, and Lady Matlock remained awake with her nephew. She watched the way Darcy's eyes continued to return to the sleeping form of Elizabeth. Whether Darcy realized his feelings or not, his aunt was well aware of his growing attachment to the young lady. Speaking softly, she captured his attention.

"Elizabeth is quite a young lady."

"She is...different."

"William, I have watched you all of your life. You have never allowed any young lady to grow so close to you, with the exception of your sister. You cannot fool me, my dear boy. It is clear to see that you care about Elizabeth."

"Aunt, with all that is happening, this conversation is inappropriate. I find Elizabeth to be a remarkable young lady, who has endured a terrible tragedy. I do not know if I would have been able to cope so well, if I were her."

"Fitzwilliam Darcy, you care for her. Admit the truth, my dear boy."

Darcy was frustrated. "Aunt, I will do no such thing. Miss Bennet is under our protection, and I would not wish for her to suffer any harm. It is my intention to see her reunited with her family."

"I find her refreshing. Can you imagine Miss Foster, or Lady Susan, if they had been forced into such a situation?" Lady Matlock smiled mischievously. "Or that sister of your friend...what is his name? Bingley?"

"Miss Caroline Bingley?" Darcy chuckled. "Heaven forbid she be forced to dress in such clothing and travel in such a manner. She would be a torture with which to make such a journey."

"To think her family is new money, and comes from trade, that woman puts on airs as if she were a member of the royal family." Lady Matlock shook her head. "Did I tell you that she was appalled to learn that she would not be invited to the ball at Fern Hall? When she approached Lady Benedict, at the modiste, she had the audacity to declare being an intimate friend of yours, not realizing I was there, and that I am your aunt."

"And what was your response to her statement?"

"Lady Benedict turned towards me, asking me if it was true, that my nephew would sink so low as to be intimate friends with such persons. I laughed lightly, and stated that you were acquainted with her, as you had attended university with her brother, but there was no intimate connection with you, as you had better taste than to align with a crass tradesman's daughter. Miss Bingley gaped like a fish on land, and it was only due to her sister taking hold of her arm, pulling her from the shop, that saved her from further embarrassment."

"I have asked Bingley to take a firm hand with his sisters, as they are both eager for Miss Bingley to make an advantageous match. For the sister, Mrs Hurst, it would relieve her from having to contend with Miss Bingley's behavior. My friend has stated that his younger sister has caused a tremendous amount of anxiety for the elder sister. Mr Hurst is displeased with Miss Bingley's behavior, so displeased that he drinks in excess to be able to be in the same room with her."

"If I were you, I would take steps to always have someone with you, when Miss Bingley is near. She is the sort who would compromise you to obtain her goal." Lady Matlock stated.

"Aunt, have no fear of anyone compromising me. From the first dance I attended, I have known the behavior of women. Not only the young ladies wishing for a wealthy husband, but their mothers who wish to have their daughters be so advantageously settled, and even the married women who wish to have a dalliance. There is always someone to avoid, and my instincts are always heightened around females."

This struck Lady Matlock as funny. Her nephew had no notion of his heart already being in danger of surrendering to the young lady with chocolate brown curls, sleeping beside him.

~~ ** ~~

"Elizabeth, we must leave." A voice spoke to her, as dreams floated at the edge of her consciousness. She was at Longbourn, with her brother and eldest sister, planning a surprise for their father's birthday.

"Not yet, Alex. We are not ready."

"Elizabeth, it is me, William. We must leave, you must come with us."

Elizabeth's eyes opened. It was not a nightmare, she was really in a barn, with people she had never met a week ago, running for her life. "What is happening?" She inquired, sleepily.

"A man was just here, speaking with the owner. He told the man that soldiers were heading this way, and they are looking for horses. We must leave now, before they arrive."

She nodded her head and began to stand, only to find his hands taking hold of her arms, pulling her lightly as he aided her to her feet. Elizabeth noticed everyone hurrying about, preparing to depart.

"We will eat on the way." Klarissa was speaking with her son, as Darcy and Elizabeth approached. "We have enough food, though we will need to purchase more when we reach Giessen."

"Mr Acker, the owner, said we should be careful, and avoid Wetzlar." Trich announced. "He said that the arch chancellor who rules there is close friends with Napoleon. We would be in extreme danger if we went to Wetzlar."

Lady Matlock turned to the man who was motioning for them to hurry, as he checked outside the door of the stables, ensuring that no soldiers were about.

They loaded the wagon and were quickly on their way, but not before Lady Matlock shook hands with the man, placing a pair of her earrings in his hands. They would give the man something to trade for whatever he needed to survive. The earrings were valuable, but not as valuable as the information that he had supplied to them.

~~~~~~~ ** ~~~~~~~

Chapter 6

Over the next two days, the wagon slowly crept across the land. The horses were tired, and would have to be traded before they reached Cologne. With soldiers about, and their desire to appropriate horses, it would be difficult to find another team.

To give the horses a bit of relief, Richard and Trich split the horses into teams. Instead of having all four horses pulling at one time, they would have one pair pulling, while the other pair walked behind the wagon. It was slower, as they did not push the horses, and, at times, the people walked beside the wagon, to lighten the load.

For Elizabeth, this was a balm to her soul. Ever since she was old enough to walk, it had been Elizabeth's way of being free from all worries. At home, she knew every inch of her father's estate by heart. Every path had been walked, every tree climbed, every stream crossed. Nothing stood in her way. The start of each day, weather permitting, was spent traipsing about the estate of Longbourn, walking to the market village of Meryton, walking to the home of her closest friend, Charlotte Lucas of

Lucas Lodge.

Her favorite place to go was to the top of Oakham Mount. From there, Elizabeth could see for miles in any direction. Alex had made it a special place for his sister, building a small bench underneath the mighty oak tree which stood alone on the hill. That had been her birthday gift, he had given her before they had left on their holiday. The memory of how happy Alex had been, when he and Jane showed it to her, was now bittersweet. Her brother had given her a treasure, a constant reminder of his love for her. There would never be a moment that she would sit on the bench and not remember his love.

Walking beside the wagon also gave her a chance to think of how she would inform her family of her brother's death. Elizabeth was certain that her mother would blame her for Alex dying. No matter what was said, Fanny Bennet would be devastated, as Alex was the heir to Longbourn. There had been talk a few years previous, when Lydia had asked what would have happened if Alex had not been born. The next male in line would be a distant cousin, a man who had had a bitter argument with Mr Bennet when they were younger, causing a rift to develop between the two families. Would this man now stand to inherit the estate, when Mr Bennet left the world behind?

Besides their parents, Jane would feel the loss of

Alex greatly. She never though ill of anyone, so how could she think ill of anyone for killing her beloved elder brother? It would be difficult for Jane, especially since she did not share her true feelings to anyone, with the exception of Alex and Elizabeth.

Their middle sister, Mary, would likely speak of their brother being in God's care. But Elizabeth did not wish to hear such words, not when the pain was so fresh.

The twins, Elizabeth had no doubts that Kitty would miss Alex, but Lydia would likely be pleased not to have their elder brother tattling on her misdeeds. Every time she got into mischief, Alex would reprimand her or take the matter to their parents. Lydia was overheard many times speaking of how angry she was with their brother. And there were even times that Lydia had shouted that she would have been happier if she did not have a brother.

"Elizabeth, are you well?" Darcy asked. He had been watching her carefully, and noticed her vacant expression.

She turned her face towards him. "I...I am fine. Forgive me. I have been woolgathering."

"If you care to share, I am happy to listen."

He was rewarded with a smile. Elizabeth thought for a moment before she spoke. "I was thinking about my family. I can picture how each are going to react to Alex's death."

"I wish we could have saved him. Losing someone you hold dear can cause a hole in one's life. Would it comfort you to speak of your brother?"

After a few moments of silence, Elizabeth glanced ahead at the path they were taking. "Alex was dear to me, as we were much alike. He preferred to be outdoors, spending as much time outside at home. I can remember Alex telling me that the only thing he disliked about going to school was not being able to enjoy the grounds like he did when he was at home. It was never a shock to find my brother reading a book while he was perched in a tree, or lying on the grass beside the river. Just before we left for Vienna, my brother gifted me with my present. My favorite place to go is the top of Oakham Mount. It is situated near two miles from our home, and from the top, I can look out over our neighborhood. The world has always looked so comforting and beautiful from the top. Alex built a bench for me, so I can sit up there, under the tree, and read. Mamma always chastises me when I sit on the ground and my dress would get dirtied."

Darcy smiled at the memory she was sharing. "I have had many lectures from my valet about grass stains on my breeches. He does not appreciate my desire to sit on the ground and enjoy the day."

"Ah, a man who would have been a like mind with Alex." Elizabeth chuckled. "I will have the bench to remind me of my dear brother. He was always thinking of me."

"Tell me about your father's estate. Is it large?"

"One of the largest in the neighborhood. The only estate larger is the one to the east of Longbourn. It is called Netherfield Park. The owners have not lived there for several years now, as Sir Henry Dempsey is elderly, and moved to York to live with his daughter's family. Our estate shares the village of Karpton, where most of our tenants live. Then the market town of Meryton, and Longbourn village, where most of our servants live. Longbourn brings in slightly over three thousand per annum. And Papa has invested with my uncle's business in Town."

"Do you know the tenants well?" Lady Matlock asked, as she decided to join the discussion. She wished to know all there was about the young lady and her family.

"Indeed. Papa and Mamma have always believed that we treat our tenants and servants with respect and dignity. My sisters and I assist Mamma in making clothes for the children, and we visit the homes every week. Many of the visits include our taking items to them, such as food, or medicine. And we do what we can to assist them."

"Your parents are wise. My husband and I believe the same, and have taught our sons the same." Klarissa spoke with pride. "William's father also believes the same. Before his mother's death, Lady Anne was frequently visiting the tenants and the village. Unfortunately, my husband's elder sister, Catherine, does not agree with such standards. It is her belief that her tenants and servants are fortunate enough to be under her protection, therefore she need not do anything further for them."

Darcy nodded in agreement with his aunt. "Mother always stated she did not know how Aunt Catherine ended up as she did, for our grandparents taught her to respect those who work to make our lives better."

"My husband has teased many times that Catherine was dropped on her head when she was an infant. It must have caused permanent damage." Klarissa teased.

Richard chimed in with his opinion, declaring that if his father was correct, his aunt must have fallen from quite some height. The conversation lightened the mood of the weary travelers, making them forget, even if only for a moment, the situation they were facing.

~~ ** ~~

Emily noticed that Thomas was somewhat warm when she tended his needs. They had been resting beneath some trees in an area where they were somewhat hidden from the world. Thomas had been fussy earlier, but he was easily soothed by Elizabeth holding him in her arms and singing softly to him. The two little girls were becoming fussy as well, so it had been accepted that the children were ready for the journey to be at an end. It was a sentiment that was shared by the adults, though they were not permitted to behave as the children did.

The decision had been made to remain hidden away until the following morning. They were nearly halfway to Giessen, and the horses would not be able to survive if they were not rested.

"What do you know of Giessen?" Elizabeth asked, trying to learn more of the area as they made their escape.

Emily had always wished to visit the city, as she wished to visit the botanical gardens that were found there. "Their botanical gardens are the oldest known, and have been kept beautiful, no matter what has happed in the area. A friend of mine told me of seeing the variety of flowers and plants they have there. She said her father would have loved to sneak in and collect cuttings from many of their plants, so he could make his own gardens."

"Is it not a part of the University of Giessen?" Klarissa asked.

"Yes, Akademischer Forstgarten GieBen is part of the Univeristy, though there is also Botanischer Garten der Justus-Liebig-Universitat GieBen, which was the oldest gardens." Trich answered. "I know of a family who used to live there, as the husband was a professor at the university."

"Would they still be there? Do you know how to find them?" Richard asked. They had been fortunate so far in the journey, though knowing someone might give them some added protection in the days ahead.

"The husband died, two years ago. The wife moved with her son's family, near our farm. They can do nothing for us."

All were saddened by the news. Klarissa packed most of their belongings back on the wagon, before settling down beside Elizabeth, who had rolled out her bedding on the ground. The two ladies had decided to share their bedding, placing one blanket on the ground, and using one to cover them. Though there was a slight chill in the air, the two were able to keep warm as they snuggled close, with Thomas between them. There would be no campfire, as such would give away their location.

Near the ladies were Richard and William on one side, and Emily, Trich and their children on the other. Each of the men took turns watching over their makeshift family. And each of the men were able to sleep several hours, giving them all renewed energy.

~~ ** ~~

When everyone woke in the morning, Elizabeth was surprised to find Thomas running a fever. The child was lethargic, sweat beading on his forehead. With water that the men had brought from a nearby stream, Elizabeth used cloths to bathe the small boy, in attempt to lower his fever.

The wagon was prepared, and everyone climbed on, ready for another days journey. Thomas continued to burn, and a cough developed by midday. Effort was made to keep Thomas separate from the other children, though it was no surprise when Gretchen became feverish later in the day. Brigit began coughing by the end of the day, just as they arrived at Giessen.

It was decided to drive the wagon around to the north side of the city, looking for a barn or stable where they could hide for the night. They hoped there would be other horses, as one of the team was beginning to limp slightly.

Finding a house with a barn, Trich and Klarissa were able to convince the family to allow them to stay. The cost was high, but they all knew how dangerous it would be, especially if soldiers found them.

The house was big enough to encompass the family of eight who lived there. The husband, Erik, worked for the blacksmith, while his wife, Margit, took in laundry for the nearby inn. Their five children, and Margit's sickly grandmother lived in the house, doing what they could to assist with the work.

"Do you know anyone who has horses for sale?" Trich inquired. "We are on our way to Cologne, and our horses need to be exchanged."

"I can ask about in the morning." Erik stated. "There is a stable about a mile from here, they may have some to sell. With everyone needing horses, they may come at a high price."

"We will take each step as it comes." Klarissa said. "Is there somewhere I can purchase supplies? We need food and such, for the remainder of the journey."

"There is a mercantile two blocks from here. My eldest son can take you there in the morning. He can carry your purchases back for you." Erik stated, placing his hands on the shoulder of his ten-year-old son. "This is Liam. He is strong, and a good boy. He will help you."

Margit walked over towards Elizabeth, who was still sitting on the bed of the wagon, holding Thomas in her arms, attempting to soothe the child. "The child, is ill?"

Elizabeth nodded her head. "We will keep him from your family. Please, do not ask us to leave." Tears were beginning to flow down her cheek.

"No, no, we not make you go. The child has fever? Any spots?"

"No spots. Cough, fever."

Margit nodded her head. "I have medicine. I bring it to you."

Before Elizabeth could utter another word, Margit hurried to her house. Several moments passed before the door opened again, and the lady was returning, with a bottle of elixir in her hand.

"This will help, works good. My children, they were sick not long ago. This made them better."

"I cannot tell you how grateful I am." Elizabeth said, taking the bottle from Margit's hands.

"You take some too, so you do not become sick. Taking care of child, you make yourself sick if not careful."

Elizabeth gave each of the children a dose of the medication. She knew they would have to use the medication sparingly, as the bottle was only partially filled. "Perhaps we should see if another bottle of the medicine can be purchased. We would not like to run out of the medicine while we are away from any apothecary."

Darcy agreed. They gave Margit the funds to purchase another bottle, suggesting she tell the physician that she wished to be prepared.

That night, the group remained in the barn, though they enjoyed their first cooked meal since they left Vienna. They enjoyed speaking with the family, as Erik and Margit were able to speak openly of their neighborhood.

It was learned that the French army had been in the area periodically, and when they were, the citizens were treated poorly. The main problem was that the Archchancellor ruling Wetzlar gave the French army preference over the citizens of the city, and the army took advantage of the fact. Those who lived in Wetzlar were fearful of being murdered or that the army would confiscate everything they owned, leaving the citizens with nothing.

Richard was thinking with military precision. He had studied to take his place with the British army, which he was scheduled to do within a month of returning from the continent. "Who is the ruler in Wetzlar"

"The Archchancellor Karl Theodor Anton Maria von Dalberg. He is also known as the Prince Bishop of Worms and Bishop of Konstanz. It is well known that he is close friends with Napoleon. You must stay away from Wetzlar." Erik warned.

Margit was concerned. "Would it be better to journey further north, rather than go to Cologne?"

The men spoke openly, and Trich went to the barn, returning with his map. Erik was showing some options they would have to avoid the French army.

"You could go through Marburg, then to Dortmund. This would put you on the path to Muster or Osnabruck. To be honest, I would go by way of Hannover. I have two brothers who were in Hannover. The people there have not been as accepting of Napoleon's ways and his army. There are more who are sympathetic to the English." Erik stated.

"Are they part of the King's German Legion?"

Richard asked, causing curious looks from his family and friends, and surprise from Erik and Margit.

"You know of the Legion?" Erik asked.

"I join the regulars upon my return from this holiday. I will be a captain. And I have been taught by some of the best minds when it comes to the military." Richard announced proudly.

"Yes, my brothers are part of the Legion. We must keep their whereabouts secret, or we would be condemned as traitors." Erik said.

Trich was uncertain of what they were speaking. "Are there forces here, who are fighting against Napoleon? I did not think there was any resistance to the French."

"They are Germans who fled to England, and are feeding information to His Majesty's army. With their knowledge of this area, and of the soldiers, they are assisting the British army." Margit stated, showing a bit of fear, mixed with great pride. "Erik's brothers are brave to join the Legion."

"If it is unsafe for you here, you should join us." Klarissa remarked. "You could travel with us. Between you and Trich, we would be safer, as you could speak for us. Though I am fluent, and my children can speak the language enough to get by as tourists, we are easily detected as foreigners."

Erik and Margit looked at each other. With tears in her eyes, Margit shook her head. "My grandmother, she would be unable to make such a journey. And the children, we would have a difficult time taking all of us. We do not even own a wagon that would be large enough to carry us."

"Margit…I wish to speak to you." Her grandmother, Hilda, announced.

"Oma, you should be resting." Margit said, walking over to the doorway, where her grandmother was standing.

"Margit, you must go with these people. You, your children, the last of our blood line. You must do this for me, for your parents. I will be able to make the journey. I am a tough old woman."

"It would kill you Oma. You know the journey would be too difficult for you."

Hilda reached over and wiped the tears with her thumbs. "I promised your grossvater that you would have a good life. After your parents died from the fever, there was only you to carry on our family. He would be disappointed in me if I kept you from flourishing. And he would be disappointed if I did not do all I could to make the journey. We will go. God has sent us angels to help us to freedom, it would be of no good to turn away from them."

And so the plans were once again altered. And more people were to join in the journey. The men continued to discuss the plans throughout the evening, even after the women and children had retired. The decision was made for Erik and Trich to make the purchases that would be needed to supply the convoy, including a wagon and horses that would be required. The two men were gone for several hours, having gone to several places, to keep from appearing suspicious.

They returned to the house in the afternoon, with not one, but two wagons and teams to pull them both. Another team of horses had been purchased in the morning, in trade for the team that had served loyally from Bamberg.

With the extra wagon, they would be able to carry some trunks, giving the appearance of a family moving from one city to another. And it would give enough room for all of the travelers to sit, especially for the children, who would easily become restless.

Fortunately, Thomas and Gretchen had begun to improve, thanks to the medicine they had been given. Margit had purchased another bottle of the concoction from the apothecary, stating she preferred to keep a bottle on hand. With five children, it was not uncommon for one child to be recovering, only to have another become ill.

That night, discussions were had for the route, where they would stop each day, possible assistance for any needs they would have. The decision was made to leave before sunrise the following morning. Trunks were packed with bedding, some keepsakes, and cooking supplies. Water was gathered in canteens, flasks, and bottles. Food was loaded on the wagon in crates and cloth sacks.

At five the following morning, three wagons left the neighborhood, taking with them seventeen people who were looking to escape the grasp of Napoleon and his army.

~~~~~~~ ** ~~~~~~~

Chapter 7

The week was long and filled with danger. Each day, the men took turns driving the teams of horses, leaving one man to rest. Near the end of the week, Klarissa decided to take a turn at the reins.

"Mother, it is inappropriate for a countess to be driving a team of horses, like a farmer's wife." Richard was shocked.

"Richard, I am your mother, Mistress of your father's homes, and can plan an elaborate dinner party or ball for the *ton.* But I am also a woman who grew up with three brothers, and I wished to be included in their activities. If I can handle the horses which pulled the curricle, I have no doubts I can control thesc beasts. So take your place on the wagon or walk beside, but I am taking a turn."

Knowing when to argue with his mother, and when to give in to her decision, Richard knew this was a case of the latter. Shaking his head in disbelief, he took his place on the wagon, just behind the driver's bench. It gave him some comfort that, if needed, he would be able to assist his mother.

~~ ** ~~

Elizabeth had taken a liking to the child who had been abandoned to her care. She found it soothing to have someone to love, someone who, like her, was a stranger to everyone else traveling in their group. Lady Matlock had her son and nephew, Trich and Emily were there with their family, and Erik and Margit had their family. Though Elizabeth felt blessed to have been included with these people, she shared no past with them. Little Thomas was the same, which brought a feeling of his being a kindred spirit with her.

She thought about what would happen when she arrived home. Fanny Bennet would be livid and distraught. It was almost a certainty that she would blame Elizabeth for Alex's death. Only the previous year, when Alex took a chill while outside on a walk with Elizabeth, Fanny threatened her second born daughter.

"If anything happens to Alex, if we are forced to leave our home after your father is in his grave, so help me, Elizabeth, you will be dead to me. I refuse to think of having a daughter who cares not for her family. Do you understand me?"

"Mamma, we were taking a walk. There was no indication there would be rain. Alex is usually healthy;

I am certain he will recover."

"You enjoy vexing me. I know you are determined to do anything to cause me vexation. My nerves...my poor nerves. I pray that my darling son survives your foolishness. Always traipsing about, walking all over the neighborhood. It will be the end of us. The end, you hear."

Elizabeth walked to her brother's rooms, finding Jane with him. "How is Alex?"

"He has a fever. Mr Jones came to check on him, and left some medicine for him. Mr Jones does not feel the fever is dire, as long as we keep it from raising higher. But you know Mamma. She begged Papa to send to Town for a physician, as she felt an apothecary could not know enough to tend the heir to Longbourn."

"Did Papa send for a physician?" Elizabeth was shocked.

"No, he felt that Mr Jones was appropriate, as the fever is not severe. He has faith in Mr Jones, as Papa has known the man for many years."

"Allow me to take over, so you can go to your room and rest. You were awake most of the night."

Jane chuckled lightly. "You only know I was awake due to your being awake. Should we find Mary, and *have her sit with Alex so that we can both rest?"*

Elizabeth agreed. As she exited the bedchambers of her brother, Elizabeth looked around, trying to find her sister. Hearing the sound of the pianoforte being played, it was no great challenge for Elizabeth to know where her sister could be found. With the music playing, and Mrs Bennet wailing, the desire to remove herself from the house played against Elizabeth's need for sleep. It was sleep which won, as she stumbled down the stairs.

"Of what are you thinking, Elizabeth?" Darcy's voice pulled her from her woolgathering.

"I was thinking of my mother, and how she is likely to treat me upon our arrival in England."

Darcy frowned. Looking ahead, he kept watch over the team of horses of which he was driving. "Will your mother not be pleased that you have survived?"

"No. My mother is not pleased with me; she never has been. I am my father's favorite, while Jane was a favorite of Mamma's. And, of course, Mamma has always held Alex dear to her heart. Now, with Alex gone, I have no delusions that Mamma will blame me for Alex's death. I wish that we could have changed places, as it would not have caused as much pain if I were the one who had been killed. It may be best that I never return home, and allow my family to believe I died as well."

"Elizabeth, please do not speak such words. What happened was terrible, but I am sure there would be just as much pain if you were lost to your family."

She lifted Thomas to her face, placing a kiss on his forehead. Tears were wet upon her cheeks, as they flowed down, dripping on Thomas' clothing. "William, my mother would disagree with you. She will force my father to expel me from our home. My best hope is that my aunt and uncle, who live in Town, will allow me to live with them. At least until I can secure employment as a governess or companion."

"No, you will not be forced to find employment. You will come to Pemberley, my father's estate. My sister, Georgiana, would be pleased to meet you, and we have plenty of room. There is no need for you to be without those who care for you."

A small gasp escaped her as she pondered his words. "Forgive me, William, it is only for our safety that your aunt deemed it necessary to pretend we are related. You owe me no such loyalty, once we leave the continent. It is me who owes you for all you have done to protect me. You have protected me, fed and sheltered me, seeing to my needs. But I was forced upon you in Vienna, and you have every right to be rid of me once we are in England."

Darcy reined in the horses, bringing them to a halt. The other wagons continued to roll forward, leaving them behind.

"Elizabeth Bennet, can you not see that I have feelings for you? Can you not understand that all I have done for you is from my heart, not from duty? You are unlike all other ladies I have known. Intelligent, courageous, and able to make your own decisions, rather than accepting mine or others to rule over your opinions. It is poor timing, I know. You are in mourning for your brother, and we are fleeing for our lives. But I cannot allow another moment to pass before telling you how much I have come to love and admire you. I would find myself the most fortunate of men, if you would do me the honor of marrying me."

Elizabeth was shocked. She had feelings developing for the handsome young man from Derbyshire. He was shy, she had discovered that quality quickly. When he was uncomfortable, a look came over his face. It reminded her of someone donning a mask. Cold, unyielding, his mask of indifference had made her watch him closely.

Did she care for him enough, enough to make such a leap as to become engaged to him? She knew him to be generous, caring, even loving. Would this be enough? Would she be happy spending the rest of her life with the man? The silence between them was causing Darcy to become concerned.

Finally, Elizabeth looked up into the eyes of the young man who had just offered for her hand. There, in his brilliant blue eyes, she found her answer. "Yes, William. I will marry you."

Pride made Darcy's chest puff out. He would have his Elizabeth. She would be his wife, to love and cherish for the rest of his life. Calling out to the wagons ahead to stop, Darcy quickly jumped from his seat and gathered Elizabeth in his arms, not caring a bit for the child in her arms. "You have made me the happiest of men, Elizabeth. My Elizabeth. You will love Pemberley. It has many paths to wander about, and the library, oh the library, I may have difficulties in removing you from the library once you have seen the collection of books. It is one of the largest private libraries in all England."

The other wagons had returned to learn what was delaying Darcy's wagon. "William, is something wrong?" Richard asked.

"Wrong? How can being accepted by a most wonderful woman be wrong? Elizabeth has agreed to be my wife." He placed a kiss on her forehead.

Klarissa smiled. "I knew you would be smart enough to make such a decision. Congratulations. Elizabeth, I am so pleased to know you will be a part of our family."

"I am pleased for your news, but we need to keep moving." Erik stated. "We can celebrate when we camp for the night."

Richard nodded his head in agreement. "Come, let us continue our journey. And welcome, Elizabeth. You will make a wonderful addition to our family."

~~ ** ~~

Mr Thomas Bennet was seated in his favorite chair near the fireplace, in his study at Longbourn. He had always enjoyed spending his days at leisure, in his study, with a good book and a glass of port. It pleased him to have a quiet home, as his wife and daughters were off visiting Fanny's sister in Meryton.

A knock on his study door broke into the attention to his book. "Enter." He called out.

The door opened to allow the housekeeper to step inside. "There is an express for you, Mr Bennet. The rider said he was told there was no need to wait for a reply."

Mr Bennet nodded his head as he took the missive. The handwriting was familiar, belonging to his wife's younger brother, Edward Gardiner, who lived in Town.

Breaking the seal, Thomas Bennet read the words.

Thomas,

I just received word from one of my suppliers, announcing that the French have attacked Vienna. I know that Alex and Lizzy are visiting my brother, so I thought I should inform you of the possibility that they have been captured or injured. From what I was able to learn, it was a quick attack, surprising most. My supplier came from Spain. He learned of the attack from a man who escaped through Elbe. It was his information that most who were attempting to escape were headed towards the Danube River, which would put them in harm's way, as the French have a strong hold in the area of Prussia and Germany.

I will keep you updated on any news that I receive. According to my supplier, it has been nearly three weeks since the attack began. There has been no news from my brother, though I pray they are all safe.

Helen and I will continue to pray for my brother and your children to be safe and on their way to England. Please inform us if you receive word from them.

Your brother,

E Gardiner

Mr Bennet was dumbstruck. His heart clutched in his chest, as the thought of losing his beloved daughter and his heir was painful. He called out to his housekeeper to come, as he felt his strength beginning to wane.

Mrs Hill entered the room, seeing her master's face becoming pale. "Mr Bennet, what is wrong? What has happened?"

"My children...my Lizzy...Alex...my children..." as Mr Bennet slouched in his chair, unable to speak any more.

Mrs Hill called for her husband, who was Mr Bennet's valet and acted as butler. "What has happened?"

"I believe he has had an attack of apoplexy. He

had just read the express that I brought him." Mrs Hill spied the message, which had fallen to the floor.

Her husband picked up the parchment, reading over what Mr Gardiner had announced. "Good God, Miss Lizzy and Master Alex are in danger. There has been an attack on Vienna, by the French. No wonder Mr Bennet had an attack, the news is horrible."

Tears were welling in Mrs Hill's eyes. She and her husband were fond of the Bennet children, but mostly fond of the eldest three. Mrs Bennet had a habit of indulging the twins with whatever they desired, and completely ignored Mary, being the middle daughter.

"You should send for the apothecary." Mrs Hill stated. "And have one of the stable hands come to assist you in taking Mr Bennet to his bed."

Mr Hill nodded his head. "After Mr Jones determines what is wrong, we should send word to Mr Gardiner."

"Indeed, for Mrs Bennet will be overcome with vapors when she hears such news."

~~ ** ~~

Gerald Darcy was in the study of his townhouse in London when the footman announced a visitor. Lord Matlock, Henry Fitzwilliam, entered the room.

"Henry, what the devil are you doing here? I thought you were at your estate."

"Matlock is running well, so I thought I would come to Town. The estate is somewhat lonely with Klarissa away."

"Part of me wishes I had taken Georgiana and joined your wife and our boys on the journey. I have never been to Vienna, and have desired to visit the city."

"Then why did you stay?" Lord Matlock inquired.

"I had several meetings that could not wait, one of which is this morning. I have someone coming here shortly, to discuss a business opportunity."

"Anything in which I would be interested? You know I am always looking for a good investment."

Gerald Darcy smiled. "Well, I suggest you remain for the meeting. I am certain that you will be welcome."

"Who is the man you are to meet?"

"Mr Edward Gardiner, of Gardiner Imports. He is expanding his business, and is looking for partners to assist with the finances. From what I have learned, Mr Gardiner is well known to have the Midas touch when it comes to business opportunities. He has made quite a fortune of his own, and is even interested in purchasing some land of his own. His wife was from Lambton. Do you remember Mr Linton, the physician?" Seeing his brother in law nod his head, Gerald continued. "Mr Gardiner's wife is the former Miss Helen Linton. She assisted Anne through Georgiana's birth, coming with her father and mother, who was the midwife. I remember the kindness that Mrs Gardiner gave my dear wife."

"If only Anne had more time with her family." Lord Matlock glanced down at the glass he had received from Gerald, filled with brandy. "My sister deserved to have had time with her daughter, with all of you. William was old enough to remember her, though just barely. I miss Anne so much. If only it had been Catherine instead."

"I agree with you whole heartedly on that sentiment." Gerald said, taking a sip of his own glass..

A knock was heard and Mr Darcy begged the person to enter. The footman announced Edward Gardiner's arrival.

Gerald and Lord Matlock stood, welcoming Mr Gardiner to the study.

"Forgive me, Mr Darcy, I was not certain that I would be able to make the appointment today, as we received some terrible news."

"What has happened?" Gerald inquired.

"We learned that the French have attacked Vienna. I have a brother living there, and my sister's son and one of her daughters is visiting the city. I fear for their safety."

Gerald's ears perked up as he turned his view to his brother in law. "Vienna? Are you certain that it was Vienna?"

"Indeed, I was told by a reliable source. He learned from someone who had escaped south, through Elbe. According to the man with which I spoke, most people were attempting to escape to the north, by way of the Danube."

Lord Matlock leaned forward, resting his forehead in his hands. "No, no, it cannot be true. We were told it was safe."

Mr Gardiner looked at the earl. "Is something wrong?"

Gerald spoke. "My son journeyed to Vienna with Lord Matlock's wife and second son. The boys had finished with the university, and we decided to give them a grand tour."

"My wife's family is from Vienna, Mr Gardiner. We were worried about their making the journey, though we were told several times that there was nothing to fear at the time. I need to send for my eldest son... we should hire someone to verify the truth and send assistance to bring them home."

"If you send someone, can you keep watch for my niece and nephew? Alexander and Elizabeth Bennet. My nephew recently graduated from university, so he is the same age as your sons. My niece is eight and ten." Mr Gardiner became hopeful for the first time since he had learned of the danger to his family.

"Of course." Gerald stated. "Would you mind if we reschedule our meeting, as we wish to learn more of the situation?"

"I see no difficultly in rescheduling. If you would send word to me as to when you are available, I will make sure I am available to meet with you."

~~~~~~~ ** ~~~~~~~

Chapter 8

After what seemed like a year of travel, the wagon train approached the outskirts of Hannover.

Erik had taken the lead, as he was familiar with the area. "We will head towards my brother's home, as his wife's family still live there. They will assist us, I am sure. My brother told me that we would always be welcome to come to them for refuge."

"You lead on. We will do as you suggest." Richard said from his wagon. Darcy was driving the third wagon, while Trich was resting. The children were restless, having been kept to the wagons most of the time. Even the adults were exhausted by the journey.

"When we reach my brother's home, we will need to be careful. It is possible that his home is being watched by soldiers. We will not be able to stay long, as there will be dangers for their family if we are discovered for what we are."

Elizabeth had been sleeping, while Lady Matlock was watching over little Thomas. The bond that had built between Elizabeth and the boy was strong, and Lady Matlock had allowed her natural instincts to act as a grandmother to surface. Thomas was a dear boy, and Klarissa was certain of the suffering of the mother who sacrificed by giving him to someone who stood a better chance to protect him. Emily was tending to her babe when she noticed what appeared to be riders coming from behind the wagons.

"Trich, look...someone is coming."

Her husband lifted his head, shading his eyes to give him a better view. "Soldiers...it is soldiers..."

Everyone was awake and nervous as they watched the troop of calvary approach them. Erik was the first to have contact with soldiers.

Speaking in broken French, Erik answered their questions, explaining that they were a family who were moving to Hannover to take care of a family farm nearby. The soldier who made it clear that he was the leader, urged his horse closer to the wagons. "You are family? One family? None of you look related."

"My wife, her grandmother, our children, my cousins, my aunt. We need to work together, as we have lost much to illness. Working together, we will be able to feed our family." Erik declared. "Our family came north, from Coburg. There was an epidemic last month. We lost many in the family. My uncle, other cousins, my father and mother. Many were lost."

"And you are all to live together?" the officer was skeptical.

"Our uncle, his sons died in an accident. He needs assistance. He has a large house, plenty big for all of us. My wife, she will take work as seamstress. My cousin, she will work at the mercantile. All is arranged. Uncle has a large barn; we will make into living areas."

"We need your wagons and horses for the army." One of the soldiers stated. "We will take them, and you walk."

"Please, we have small children and my wife's mother, she is weak. They cannot walk so far."

"You will give us the wagons and horses, or we will teach you a lesson. We will start with your wife." The officer moved closer to the wagon Erik was driving.

"Please, I beg of you. Leave us two wagons. We can make do with two wagons. I ask for our women and children." Erik pleaded.

A cold hard smack across his face was his answer. Margit cried out, wishing to move to her husband. Only his hand held out stopped her. Erik looked into his wife's eyes, willing her to calm.

"Sir, I beg of you, we cannot continue on by foot. The distance is too great. Please, can you allow us one of the wagons? Just one of the wagons, with a team of horses. The strong ones can walk, while the weaker ones will be able to ride. Please, I beg you." Erik pleaded, standing tall in front of the officer who struck him.

"We could kill you all, and take the wagons."

"Indeed, you could. But showing us compassion will be better for all. You would wish cooperation from the citizens in this neighborhood. If you show us kindness, we can sing your praises to everyone. It will show everyone that you are willing to be generous rather than cruel."

One of the lower ranked officers moved forward, coming alongside the senior officer. After several moments of whispering behind their hands, the two men came to an agreement.

"One wagon and horses. Everyone off the other two wagons. Quickly...quickly... or we will make you move faster." The officer declared. To make his point, he took his crop and swung it, striking Darcy on his cheek. Elizabeth cried out, frightened by what she was witnessing, especially as it was Darcy who was injured. Everyone moved, as quickly as possible, placing the women and children on the wagon that

Erik was driving. Richard took the seat next to Erik, as he stayed alert to the soldiers.

"You, you look strong. We need workers for the army. You would do nicely to do hauling of supplies." The officer was looking at Richard.

Klarissa spoke. "He is my son, Sir. And he is deaf. He cannot hear you, and would not be able to understand you. The fever, it left him in such a sad way. Please, my husband is gone, and my sons have promised we will stay together." Pointing at Darcy, she continued. "My other son, he has a weak heart. He looks strong, but cannot work hard. He takes care of the animals, he and his wife, and their babe. Take the wagons, but leave our family together. I beg of you."

Real tears were streaming from Klarissa's eyes, dripping off her jaw. Elizabeth took hold of Darcy's arm, holding him tightly to her, while she held Thomas in her other arm. She prayed that the soldiers would forget about the people and would take only the two wagons with only the horses that were attached to them.

Several moments passed before the officer in charge moved forward. "Leave now, before I change my mind. Go, or I will take the men and all the wagons and horses."

Darcy sat on the very end of the wagon, with Trich beside him, both dangling their legs off the wagon. The soldiers took possession of the other wagons and headed them in a different direction. Once they were far enough away from the soldiers, everyone was able to breathe again.

Richard looked at his mother. "You were quite clever, old girl. What made you think of such a rouse?"

"I had to come up with some reason why you would not be a good servant for them. To look at you, there is no obvious defect. But hearing would be a distinct problem. And a weak heart, which could cause someone to die if overworked, was another difficulty."

"I am proud to call you my mother." Richard declared, a smile on his face. "It is one story I will have to write down, for I will need to share this with any children with which I am blessed."

~~ ** ~~

The lone wagon finally arrived at Erik's relations. The family quickly took them in their house, hiding the wagon and horses as quickly as possible. Erik's sister in law's father was concerned.

"Since your brothers left, we have had soldiers

coming here regularly to see if they can find them here. They believe we are hiding them."

"We did not know. Will you be in danger having us here?" Erik asked nervously.

"Perhaps. They will wish to take you men, to work for them. And the horses will be taken immediately. We have had no horses to work the farms for over a month."

"Can you find assistance for us to reach the coast? We are heading for England."

The elder man looked Erik over. "I am surprised to see you abandoning your homeland."

"I will not fight for the French, nor will I allow them to kill me in front of my wife and children. Word reached our neighborhood that my brother had fled from French troops. We were in danger if we remained."

"You are much like your brother. We have had no word from him or our daughter. We pray every day to have word that they are safe and have found peace wherever, in their new home."

"We will leave as soon as possible. Can you assist us in purchasing more supplies? The soldiers we dealt with took our other wagons and horses. The poor beasts we have left are exhausted."

"The horses will have to make do for now, as I can assure you there are none available that the French forces have not taken by force. Perhaps a day of rest will allow them to recover enough to continue the journey. Supplies, I am not sure. I will send word to my son, have him come to dine with us. He would be able to tell us the best alternatives for you to continue your journey."

"Many thanks, Abel. We will never forget your kindness."

~~ ** ~~

When Abel's son, Rainhardt, arrived, it was learned that the young man was in contact with a network of people who assisted others to escape from Napoleon's forces.

"When I received my father's message, I sent word to some men who assisted my sister and your brother." Rainhardt announced to Erik. "I asked them to join us after dinner. They will have the best information on making the journey. I wish we could convince my parents to leave. It will be safer for our family to be away from here."

"Your mother will never leave here. Her parents are buried near the farm, she will never go to live in another country." Abel replied. "And I will never leave your mother."

"It is not safe. The French soldiers are aware that our sister and her husband escaped. How many times have the soldiers come to search your home for them? They purposely steal items from you, or break items they do not wish to steal. It is a miracle they have not done worse to you. Mr Hoffman was beaten near death after his son escaped."

"They will not harm me. So long as we do not give them any cause, they will leave us be."

Rainhardt shook his head. He knew his father would continue to live his life as though all was normal. The soldiers were causing so much trouble, looting, taking anything they wished, even burning down homes and barns. A butcher who had been in their neighborhood for more than twenty years, had recently been ruined when the soldiers took all of his meat from the shop, then set fire to the shop. The only reason for the destruction was that his nephew, who had worked at the shop, had left with Erik's brother.

The dinner was a simple repast, with stew, bread, and cheese. Lady Matlock laughed to herself when she thought about her waist line. She knew she had added several inches to her girth over the past years, but this trip had gone a long way in slimming her down. She would have to refrain from over indulgence when they returned to England.

When the men arrived, it was discovered that they were planning to assist a small group of Hannover soldiers through their network of safe homes, taking them to Emden. The coastal city was a part of Holland, and was friendly with England. Once there, it would be simple enough to find a ship sailing to England. The men stated that it would take a week for them to make the journey, as they could only travel certain roads, at certain times. They had soldiers at checkpoints who were loyal to Hannover and their people.

"Will you have money or items that you can exchange for services of those who place themselves in danger to aid you?" one of the men asked the group.

Lady Matlock looked at Darcy, nodding her head slightly. Darcy spoke for his relations. "We have the funds to pay for all of us to make the journey. If what we have is not enough, we can get more when we are in friendly territory."

"It will be dangerous, with such a large group. The women will be in the most danger, as the soldiers are fond of enjoying our local ladies. Many young lady has been ruined in just a year's time. Do not let me frighten you ladies, but you must be aware of what might happen."

"Have no fear for us." Lady Matlock stated, her chin held high. "We will do as we are told, so we are not captured by Napoleon's minions."

"Then we will leave tomorrow evening. You will need to keep yourself out of sight during the day, and keep as quiet as possible, as you do not wish to drawn attention to your being here."

"What about the horses and wagon?" Erik inquired.

"We will take them with us tonight. They will be valuable to us."

Darcy and Richard looked from Erik and Trich to the other men. Losing their last method of transportation was difficult, not knowing these other men could guarantee their safety. Finally, Lady Matlock spoke. "We are placing our very lives in your hands, gentlemen. If the horses and wagon can benefit you in your work, they are yours."

"You have our word, we will do all we can to take you to safety. We may have to take you in smaller groups, as it is less likely to be caught. Are you willing to split into smaller groups?"

All of the adults nodded their heads. One of the men came up with anidea. "Perhaps we could take the children with one or two of the ladies with us. If we are questioned, we could claim that we were taking the children to the orphanage in Nienburg. Everyone is aware the orphanages here are filled, and there has been a new one established in Nienburg. We could take them on the wagon, make it appear we had been hired to transport them to the new building."

The idea was sound, though it was difficult for the two mothers to imagine trusting their children into the care of these unknown men. It was decided that Hilda, Elizabeth and Klarissa would be the females to ride with the children, as the children would not be likely to refer to them as their mothers. The probability of the children slipping up with their mothers was high. The children referring to Hilda as Oma, or grandmother, would be a term of endearment that was frequently used towards an elderly woman, whether or not she was a grandmother.

So it was decided, and plans were made for the following day. The women would instruct the older children in the morning, teaching them how they should behave if need came.

Though they felt safe in the attic of Abraham's home, it was still difficult to sleep, knowing what faced them on the morrow.

Chapter 9

The men arrived in the middle of the afternoon the following day. They had decided it would be best to move the children, Hilda, Elizabeth and Klarissa while there was still light outside. All of the men and the other ladies would have to be taken after dark.

The men who would take the first load were a pair of brothers named Jorn and Werner. Klarissa smiled. "How appropriate that we rest our safety in brothers whose names mean vigilant watchman and defending warrior. I feel safer already."

This made the brothers smile. Jorn spoke. "Our mother said there was a reason we were named such, and we should always watch over and protect those in need. You are most certainly in need."

"I am Klarissa, and this is my daughter, Elizabeth. We will be taking charge of the children."

"We have a sister named Ellyzabeth. It means God's oath. She will be meeting us at our first stop. Her husband is joining us as well, as the two of them will aid you to the second stop." Werner said. "We should load everyone quickly, and make a show of thanking Abel for assisting the orphanage. This will assist in protecting the family from nosey neighbors."

The ladies rounded up all of the children, and led them outside to the wagon. Klarissa and Jorn made a show of thanking Abel, shaking his hand as they spoke.

"The orphanage is grateful for your kindness. With so many children coming there, we had nowhere to house them overnight. The journey to Nienburg will be better, now that the children have had a good meal and rest." Klarissa stated fluently. No one would ever guess that she had lived in England for the last thirty years of her life, speaking little of her native language.

"Always a pleasure to assist the children." Abel said. "My wife will miss the children, as she is quite fond of little ones. It is sad that so many have been left without family to love them."

"We will send word if we require your assistance again. If you wish, we would always welcome your visiting us in Nienburg. The new orphanage will need people willing to comfort the children." Klarissa stated. In doing so, she left the opening for a plausible reason Abel and his wife would leave their home without speculation from neighbors.

Abel nodded his head. "Perhaps we will. If my wife is willing."

"You are always welcome."

With that, Klarissa joined Elizabeth, Hilda, and the children on the bed of the wagon. As they pulled away, Klarissa began singing a children's song, encouraging the elder children to join her. Elizabeth held Thomas in one arm, and Gretchen in her other, while Klarissa sat like a mother bird with her wings spread out, tucking the other children in protectively, while Hilda sat holding the hand of Liam, her eldest grandson. His father had instructed the boy to keep a watch over his grandmother and siblings, and Liam intended to be the man of the group.

The wagon was stopped several times, soldiers who wished to know where the wagon was traveling. One officer felt the children should be made to walk, as the officer wished to commandeer the wagon. It took some quick thinking on Jorn's part to dissuade the man.

"We have infants and an elderly woman who is like a grandmother to the children. If we were to walk to Nienburg, it would surely take her life. The children have lost so much, please do not take away a kind woman who has opened her heart to them." As the officer was about to argue, a superior officer approached.

"What is happening?" the man asked.

"They do not need the wagon and horses, and we need them to move the supplies to the troops to the south. The children can walk the distance to the orphanage." The first officer stated, certain his superior would approve of his decision.

Jorn directed his attention to the new officer. "We are on our way to Nienburg, to the new orphanage. These children, including infants, have lost their homes and families, and now are being moved to another orphanage, because of the ones here in Hannover being full. We were hired to take them and these ladies, who have volunteered to care for the children, to their new home. The one lady is elderly, and she is too weak to walk such a distance. The children call her Oma, as she has become a grandmother to all of them. Please, I beg of you, do not take away our transportation. It would be as if you killed her before their eyes.

Wishing to do his part to protect his family, Liam, began crying. "Not Oma, please, not Oma. She is a good lady. She cannot walk far. Please, Oma cares for us." He had pinched himself hard, in effort to bring tears to his eyes.

The superior officer looked over the wagon bed,

taking in all the children. "Go then, we will allow you to keep your wagon and horses."

"But…"

"Did you not hear my orders?" the officer barked at his junior officer's reluctance.

"Y…yes sir." The junior officer looked at Jorn and sneered. "As he said, go on. But if I see you again, the wagon and the horses are mine."

Jorn nodded his head and motioned to his brother to start the horses moving. Once they were far enough from the officers, Hilda leaned over and placed a kiss on her great grandson's head. "Liam, you did a good deed. Your parents will be proud of your actions."

"I was told to protect you and the other children, I was only doing as my father told me." Liam said, trying not to show his pride in his performance.

Elizabeth smiled and Klarissa nodded her head. "Your parents will be proud of your acting. You made the men see you as children, not just a wagon they could confiscate. Your young voice, crying out to protect your grandmother, saved us all from losing our transportation."

The words from Klarissa made the young boy

realize how valuable he had been. This brought him to sit a little prouder and squeeze his grandmother's hand.

~~ ** ~~

The group came to a farm house that was five miles south of Nienburg. There, the ladies were welcomed to bring the children inside the small house, where Ellyzabeth and her husband, Garon, were waiting for them. Jorn and Werner would remain at their farm, working for the couple, while Ellyzabeth and Garon took the group to the next stop.

While they were at the farm, they would be fed and rest until the other members of their group arrived in the morning. Liam made his siblings mind their manners, thanking their hosts for their kindness. Hilda was proud of her great grandchildren, as they were being strong in the face of all the terror around them.

The children slept soundly, with the farm being quiet and calm. The ladies spoke with the family, as Werner and his sister detailed the rest of the journey, where they would stop, what precautions had been taken, what potential threats could still be before them. Though they were far from being free from danger, Elizabeth and Klarissa felt there was light at the end of the tunnel. They would be to Emden and on a ship, bound for home, in less than a fortnight. And Elizabeth would be with William, as they prepared for a future life together. As she drifted off to sleep, Elizabeth wondered if Alex would have liked Fitzwilliam Darcy, and if he would have approved of her engagement to the man. It was not official, as William had not been given permission by Mr Bennet, but Elizabeth was certain that her father would approve of the young man to whom his treasured daughter had given her heart.

~~ ** ~~

The following day, near midmorning, the remaining members arrived, usually in small groups of three or four people. There had been six men and women who had served as escorts. They quickly ate the food that was given them, and were on their way back to Hannover. There were more people in need of their services.

As soon as Darcy spied Elizabeth, he gathered her in his arms. "Thank heavens you are safe." He whispered in her ear. "I have been worried about you since you left Abel's home."

"We are all safe. We had very little trouble, and our guides were masterful at speaking to the soldiers."

"You were stopped?" Darcy pulled back slightly,

looking her over, as if to make certain she had no visible injuries.

Elizabeth smiled. "As you can see, I am unharmed. As are the rest of our group. Liam should be commended for his performance when we needed to tug on the hearts of an officer."

"There were no real difficulties, William, and I am well. Thank you for taking the time to notice." Klarissa said with a chuckle.

"Forgive me, my thoughts were carried away with all sorts of possibilities. It was the longest day and night of my life. I am pleased that all of you are safe, and unharmed." Darcy gave his aunt a peck on the cheek. "And thank you for watching over my dearest girl."

"You are very welcome, my dear William. She has taken very good care of the children. And I must admit, she is a pleasure to be with."

Darcy smiled. "I had no doubts at all. But I am relieved to finally have her with me once again."

Everyone was inside the farm house, making for a tight squeeze.

Garon discussed the next segment of their journey, before the new arrivals were shown upstairs, to the attic, where Ellyzabeth had laid out blankets and pillows for everyone to rest. They would wait until the sun was down before she and her husband would lead the group further towards their goal.

"We will take you as far as Vechta. There are three men there who will take you on to Cloppenburg. From there, you will go to Papenburg. The men at Papenburg will take you to Emden." Garon explained to the adults. "We have made this journey many times, assisting many to escape Napoleon. The men we will pass you to are very good. Kyland, Barret, and Leonard."

Klarissa laughed. "I am beginning to think that you have all taken new names to fit your assistance in this system."

When everyone looked at her with curiosity, she explained. "I have always enjoyed learning the meaning behind names. Kyland stands for bull, Barret for being brave as a bear. Leonard is lion-hearted. And Garon, your name stands for guards. You all live up to your names, with courage and wisdom."

Ellyzabeth smiled. "My brothers were telling us that you commented on their names. I am not familiar with your name though. For what does Klarissa stand?"

Klarissa looked at her son and nephew. "Well, to

be honest, my full name is Klara Marissa, but I shortened it when I moved to England."

"Ah, Klara means bright and famous." Ellyzabeth stated. "You are bright, in personality and of mind, and I have no doubts that you are quite famous in England."

Richard was dumbstruck, never knowing his mother's name was different from what she had been called all of his life. "She is very famous, and valued as a dear friend to many."

"She is respected for her generosity and kindness." Darcy added. "And I know her opinions and advice are often sought out by others."

Klarissa was beginning to blush. "Well, enough of this foolishness. We should all rest, so we will be ready to begin again tonight."

~~ ** ~~

The remainder of their journey went without much difficulty. There were a few times they encountered people, but the further north they got, the less influence the French army had on the area. When they arrived in Emden, everyone took a deep sigh of relief. The two men and a woman who had arrived in Emden with them were Ingel, Jesaja, and Leyna. Again, Lady Matlock smiled at their names.

"Your parents named you well. Ingel means angel, and Leyna is little angel. And Jesaja means God will help. We cannot thank you enough for your care of us. All of you who are aiding others in such a manner, taking dangerous risks on behalf of others you do not know, you have been a gift from God in our time of need."

Richard and Darcy reached into their pockets to retrieve the funds they still had. Taking the coins from Darcy, Richard handed the stack to the trio. "With this, and the wagon and horses, you should be able to assist more people."

Looking at the amount they had been given, the trio were amazed. They had guessed that some of the people were well to do, but not so rich as to afford such a generous donation. Jesaja thanked Richard, nodding to Darcy as well. Turning towards the rest of the group, he spoke.

"With these funds, we will be able to assist many more people. So many of the people we have helped have very little left, having had to leave their homes and businesses behind. This is a blessing to all of them. You have the gratitude of many people."

"We did not tell anyone outside our group, for fear of what could happen if it were learned, but my mother is Lady Matlock, Countess of Matlock. I am the younger son of the Earl of Matlock, Henry Fitzwilliam. My cousin, Fitzwilliam Darcy, is heir to the largest estate in Derbyshire. When we arrive in England, we will send you more aid. Give us the name and location of someone here, in Emden, we can contact to give you further funds and other resources."

Leyna had tears streaming down her cheeks. "You cannot know how grateful you have made us. I will be staying here, with my sister, in the bakery near the docks. We will go there, to give you a meal before you board the ship. While we are at the bakery, Ingel will find which ship will be leaving today."

Lady Matlock nodded her head. As they arrived at the bakery, Elizabeth realized she still had some of the funds her brother had given her as pin money. Elizabeth had hidden the coins in her boot, so they would not be as noticeable. Sitting down at a table, Elizabeth took a quick look to ensure no one was watching. Quickly, she slipped off her boot and retrieved the coins. Before she could do anything else, Elizabeth noticed that her betrothed was watching her. His eyes were focused on her small, delicate foot. It surprised him to see such a delicate part of a young woman who had shown such strength and courage.

"Elizabeth," Darcy said, coming to sit beside her. "I know we have not discussed much beyond arriving in

England. It would be proper for me to speak with your father, as you are no yet of age. But we are not in England. And by all rights, I have compromised you multiple times. It would be proper, if we were to wed here, in Emden, before we stepped foot on the boat. Your reputation would be protected, and we would not need to separate when we arrive in England."

Elizabeth stared into his blue eyes, sparkling with the love she knew he held for her. She did not wish to be disrespectful to her parents, especially to her father. They would have a difficult time as it was, when they learned of Alex's death. Would it add to their grief to learn that Elizabeth had married without approval? She understood his view, and having to separate from him would be far too painful to endure. The longer she looked at him, the more she agreed with him. Finally, she said the words. "Yes, William, let us marry here, today."

~~~~~~~ ** ~~~~~~~

Chapter 10

"England." The word caressed Elizabeth's lips as she spied the shores of her homeland, from the deck of a merchant ship. Darcy stood beside her, holding her hand in his. Bringing her hand to his lips, he placed a gentle kiss.

"Home." He replied.

"A new home for me." Elizabeth stated, looking into the gaze of her new husband. "So many changes in so short a time."

"Your family will be joyous that you have returned. How could they not? It was a miracle that you have come through the trials we faced. Many would have collapsed under such strain."

"My mother will likely not agree with your view. I dread facing her. I dread...I can see the look my father will have when he learns that his first born and heir is dead. The pain that he will suffer tears at my heart." Elizabeth turned into her husband's embrace, her face resting on his strong chest. "What will we do with Thomas?"

"I was thinking that we would take him to Pemberley. We can accept him as our ward, or find one of the families in the neighborhood who will take him, raise him to be a fine young man."

"It is difficult to think he would not be with us every day. Please, can we keep him with us? I am aware that there will likely be talk, with him so young, and us away from England."

"But Thomas was born prior to our even leaving British soil. No one can claim him as being your natural child, and most definitely not our child." Darcy stated, holding her close.

"Facts such as those do not matter when there is a juicy bit of gossip to spread." Elizabeth sighed. "Where should we go first?"

"We arrive in London, so perhaps, to my family's townhouse. We can send word to your aunt and uncle, inviting them to visit. It would be best if we got proper rest and a good meal, before we set out for Longbourn."

Elizabeth nodded her head. In her mind, there was also a natural hesitancy about the coming night. As it had her first night of marriage while on board the sea, they had decided to wait to consummate their wedding. Darcy did not wish for their first night together to be in such a manner. "I feel as if I could sleep for a fortnight."

"I have no doubts, as I feel the same. And you have no fear that I will demand anything more from you tonight. We both have recovering to do, and I insist on your taking care of yourself."

The activity was lively, as they approached the docks of London. Lady Matlock and Richard embraced, tears freely flowing from the eyes of both.

Lady Matlock turned towards the others in their group. Addressing all of them, she spoke. "Now, keep close when we disembark. We will find transportation to take us to Matlock house. There, you will be able to take baths, eat as much as you desire, and sleep in comfortable beds. And once we are well rested, we will speak with my husband and William's father. Between the two estates, I am certain we will be able to find work and housing for everyone."

Erik and Margit held their children close, as Liam held his Oma's hand. She had surprised everyone with her strength and courage, especially after Liam's performance with the soldiers. Hilda told her granddaughter that if a lad of ten years could stand strong and protect his loved ones, she could do no less.

For Trich and Emily, there was a sense of peace. Emily was returning home, and she had family living

Leicester. She would be able to see them for the first time in six years, and introduce her children to their relations. Trich was grateful for working on the ship on the Danube, as it had brought so many new possibilities to his family.

Once the ship was secured at the docks, the passengers began to depart. Lady Matlock was surprised to hear her name called out from the crowd on shore.

"Lady Matlock, Master Richard, Master Darcy, welcome back." A young man came forward. He was recognized as one of the footmen from Matlock House.

"James, what are you doing here?" Lady Matlock asked in surprise.

"Your husband has me coming daily to check for any ships from the continent. He and Mr Darcy have been quite worried about you, since word arrived of the attack on Vienna. I dare say they will be quite relieved to have you returned."

"They had word of the attack on Vienna?" Darcy was somewhat surprised. He wondered how word had arrived before they had.

"Yes, a tradesman, with whom they were doing business, had learned from one of his suppliers of the French army invading. From what I understand, the supplier had made the journey south from Vienna, through Italy and then on the ocean."

"James, we will need several carriages to take us to the townhouse." Lady Matlock advised. "We have grown in numbers on our journey, and these fine people have made it possible for us to return. And my nephew has brought home a bride."

The footman was shocked at the information. Though his Mistress and her relations were poorly dressed, he recognized the other members of their group to be of the working class. But his Mistress had commanded him, and James went in search of carriages to convey them to their destination.

Everyone was loaded in the carriages, and what few belongings remained with them were secured on top of the carriages. Relaxing on the seat, beside her son, Lady Matlock gave a deep sigh. They were home.

"I want the staff to fill the bathing tub with hot water, and keep the hot water at the ready to replenish when the water in the tub cools. I plan to soak there for at least half a day."

Richard laughed. "I plan to have cook fix a huge meal. I might even be kind enough to share a bit of the food with others."

"Father will be pleased to see us returned. It

would not surprise me if he held a grand dinner for all of us within the next day or two." Darcy stated.

"We will need to make the journey to Hertfordshire soon. I do not wish for my family to be frightened while waiting for word. If news of the attack has reached London, I am certain my father has heard of it from the papers or from my uncle, who lives in London."

"Perhaps tomorrow, if we are able, we can make the journey." Darcy smiled at his wife, giving her hand a squeeze.

"My uncle should go with us to Longbourn. My parents will need his guidance, after they learn the news."

"I will invite him to come with us. Do not fret. You are not alone."

~~ ** ~~

James had sent a runner with a message to Matlock House, informing Lord Matlock of great news, so it was of no surprise that the earl and Gerald Darcy were coming out the door of the townhouse before the door of the carriage could even be opened. The men were surprised to see two more carriages following the one containing their relations, though they paid no mind to them, once they caught sight of their loved ones.

Darcy waited for his cousin to exit the carriage and hand his mother down. As soon as he stepped out, his father was quick to move towards him. William held up his hand stopping his father for a moment, as William turned and handed Elizabeth down. Gerald Darcy was shocked.

"Father, I wish to introduce you to my wife. Mrs Elizabeth Darcy, nee Bennet, this is my father, Mr Gerald Darcy. We were married, just before leaving Emden."

Gerald was stunned. He had never imagined his son to be impulsive, especially when it came to deciding to wed. Had a fortune hunter trapped his son into a marriage? Lady Matlock had seen the look in her brother in law's eyes, and smiled.

"Gerald, there is nothing to fear. Elizabeth is a fine young gentlelady, and I approved the marriage. Though technically, Elizabeth had been compromised throughout our journey, they married for love."

"Indeed, Father, Elizabeth is all that is good. I am certain you will approve of her, once you know her."

Elizabeth blushed at the statements being made about her. Gerald moved to stand in front of the young lady, looking deep into her eyes, as if searching her very soul for the truth of her. "Welcome, Mrs Darcy. It is a pleasure to meet you."

"I wish we had had some way to notify you, but we decided, just this morning, that we did not wish to be apart. Not after all we have been through. It is understandable that you would hold reservations about our marrying, under such circumstances." Elizabeth said, before glancing up at her husband.

The single movement, the look in her eyes, as well as the look William wore, and Gerald was certain that what he had been told was the truth.

"Come, all of you, inside. There is much to discuss, but it would be best to do so inside." Lord Matlock declared. "I have already informed the staff to prepare refreshments and heat water for baths, as I am certain you desire both."

"Husband, there are more than just us to come inside." Lady Matlock announced, motioning her head towards the group that had formed behind her. "These people have been invited to be our guests at our home and Darcy House."

Gerald and Lord Matlock were surprised, though accepted Lady Matlock's information and welcomed everyone inside. William went over to Margit, who was holding Thomas, and relieved the lady of the young boy. This caused his father's brow to lift in curiosity. It was clear to see the elder Darcy was expecting a detailed explanation from his son.

Watching his son closely, it was plain to see that William was comfortable carrying the infant, and the child seemed at ease with William. What was the story? Was the reason for the hurried wedding on the continent to cover an affair his son had while still in the university? Could this young lady have traveled to the continent to meet his son, to make their relationship appear legitimate?

Suddenly, Gerald stopped. "What did you say is your family name?"

"Bennet. I was Elizabeth Bennet, of Longbourn, in Hertfordshire."

"Your uncle . Is Edward Gardiner your uncle?"

Elizabeth's eyes grew wide. "He is. He is my mother's brother. Do you know him?"

"I do. It was through him that I learned of the invasion of Vienna. Mr Gardiner asked me to keep a watch for you and your brother." Gerald turned towards the two unknown men in their group.

Elizabeth faltered, choking on her words. William looked at his father. "Elizabeth's brother was killed in Vienna. He was shot as we were boarding a boat. His body fell into the Danube river."

Gerald could not miss the tenderness his son showed his bride, wrapping her in his embrace. The pain was obvious, and the grief was fresh for the young lady.

While they were fleeing for their lives, Elizabeth had placed her overwhelming loss on hold. Now, being in England, safe from the dangers of a warzone, the pain came crashing down on her shoulders. Quickly, her simple tears turned into sobs, as her thin body was wracked with grief.

"Can you send word to her uncle, invite him to join us?" William inquired. "There is much to discuss, before we journey to Longbourn."

"I received a message yesterday that Mr Gardiner was going to Hertfordshire and would be gone for some time. We were supposed to meet next week, so he wished to inform me that he would be unable to make the meeting."

This news frightened Elizabeth. "William, we must make the journey immediately. Something must be wrong, for Uncle to leave London. He rarely leaves his business affairs to journey to visit, only at holidays."

"Father, could we use the Darcy carriage? We may

be a few days in Hertfordshire."

"Of course, of course. Why do we not make our way to Darcy House and order the carriage readied. And you can freshen up before we make the trip."

"We?" William looked at his father.

"As it involves a member of my family, I intend to join you. And I wish to know more about your trip, and more about my new daughter."

William turned to his aunt. "Will you be able to care for our guests in our absence? I feel guilty asking you to shoulder the burden."

"Tis no burden, William. We will take care of everything here, you see to your bride." Lady Matlock stepped to the couple, placing her hands on either side of Elizabeth's face. "If we need to come to Hertfordshire, you need only send word. You have been my daughter for the past weeks, it does not end now that we are safely returned home."

"Thank you, Aunt." Elizabeth replied, allowing the motherly warmth of Lady Matlock's kiss on her forehead to envelop her.

"Do you wish for us to keep Thomas here?"

Elizabeth was unsure as to what they should do with the child. Thomas had bonded with them, having been with either Elizabeth or William since he had been hoisted into the wagon. "He is good with you and Emily. But he is to be our ward, should we not have him with us? I do not wish to cause him pain for being away from us."

"Thomas was blessed when he was entrusted into your care. He knows you love him. I am certain we can manage for a few days, and if it is too difficult, we will bring him to Hertfordshire." Lady Matlock promised.

~~ ** ~~

The journey was long in Elizabeth's opinion. The day had been filled with so many changes, and still more were to come. She knew they would arrive at Longbourn late in the day, but she could not help the time. She was certain that something terrible had happened, for her uncle would not have gone to Longbourn unless something important had happened. Elizabeth could only pray that it was not something terrible.

William and Gerald spoke freely, as the son enlightened his father of all they had endured to return home to England. Gerald was amazed that his son had arrived unharmed, as he could have just as easily been killed as Alex had been. His heart went out to his new daughter, hearing all they had been through, and Elizabeth without anyone she knew before Vienna. The gentleman's respect grew in leaps and bounds for the young lady.

"Mrs Darcy, you have my sincere condolences on your loss. I am grateful that my son and our relations were there, to be of assistance to you."

"Please, Mr Darcy, I beg of you to call me Elizabeth, or, as my family does, Lizzy."

"Then you must call me Gerald, or Father. I will do whatever I can to smooth things over with your family. Perhaps we can have a ceremony on English soil, so that both of our families can be witness. That should appease your parents, should it not?"

"The loss of my brother will cause them far too much pain to consider a wedding. We will be in full mourning for six months, then half morning." Elizabeth replied. "I knew that we would have to wait for a year before marrying, if we had waited until we arrived here only betrothed. It may sound selfish, but I have come to love and depend on your son. I cannot imagine having to be apart from him for a year."

"I am sorry you had to make such a difficult decision. It must have been painful. But I can understand your reasoning. Seeing you with my son, it is clear to see that you both love each other. We will weather this together, for you are a Darcy now."

The carriage was beginning to slow down, and Elizabeth glanced out the window. She knew they were approaching the main house of her father's home. The thought of seeing her father was soothing to her soul.

As the carriage came to a stop, one of the windows showed a curtain that had just been moved. Elizabeth knew instantly that it would be her younger sisters or their mother, peeking to see who was coming.

William stepped down from the carriage, handing down his wife. She was dressed in a gown that had been one of William's mother's, as all Elizabeth had with her was what was on her back and one other battered, tattered gown from the journey. Fortunately, she was nearly the same measurements as her deceased mother in law. Her hands instantly moved to smooth out any potential creases from the journey, though William could see that she was attempting to find something constructive to do with her hands.

Gently, he placed her hand on his arm and led her to the door. Before anyone could knock, the door opened. Mr Hill, the Bennet family butler and valet for her father, opened the door. He was amazed to see the young lady he had known all of her life. Mr Hill and his wife, who was the housekeeper, had been with Longbourn since before Elizabeth was born.

"Miss Lizzy, you have returned." The man said, emotion bubbling up in his words. "We had thought... oh, but that is not important. Is Master Alex with you? Is he in Town?"

The tears were already pooling in Elizabeth's eyes. Realizing his wife was having difficulty, William spoke. "Unfortunately, he was unable to return to England. But we should speak of this inside."

"Forgive me, please." Mr Hill could not keep his eyes from the young lady before him. "My wife will be overjoyed to see you returned, Miss Lizzy. You have been sorely missed. We feared you had been killed in Vienna."

Elizabeth understood the sentiment behind the beloved servant's words. She and Alex, along with Jane, had been the favorites of the staff and tenants.

The trio entered the house and were shown into the parlor. Jane was the first to realize that her treasured sister had returned home. Jane stood and ran across the room, wrapping Elizabeth in her arms. Darcy knew, from his wife's words, that Jane was her closest friend and cherished sister, so he was not put out when she all but dismissed him from Elizabeth's side.

"Lizzy, oh Lizzy. We have feared you lost forever. You have returned. Oh, Lizzy. I have missed you terribly. But you are here, and safe."

When the pair were finally beginning to move apart so they could look at one another, they could hear hurried footsteps on the stairs. In a moment, Mrs Bennet had joined the group, having rapidly descended from her bedchamber. "Lizzy, you are alive. Oh, goodness, we are saved. We are saved. You were not killed, as we feared. Oh, but where is Alex? I wish to see my son."

"Mamma, please, allow me to speak."

"But he must be here, if you are here. Where is my dear boy?"

"Mamma, I need to tell you..."

Mrs Bennet's eyes turned cold. "No, no no no. I will not hear you say it. You are here, so your brother must have returned home as well. I demand to see him immediately."

"Please, Mamma, I must tell you..."

They heard footsteps coming down the hall and Elizabeth turned to see her uncle entering the parlor. "Uncle, we were told you were here."

Mr Gardiner was shocked to see his niece with the Darcys. "Dearest Lizzy, you have been restored to our family. Alex, is he here as well?"

When Gardiner looked at the men who had arrived with his niece, Gerald Darcy gave a slight shake of his head.

Mrs Bennet's fury grew. "You are to blame. You should never have gone with Alex. If he had not had you for whom to care, he would be here. But you begged to go, and your father was always foolish about allowing you whatever you wished. Now what will happen? We will be thrown from our home. It is terrible, just terrible. And it is all your fault, Elizabeth." With that, Mrs Bennet's hand flew quickly, striking her second eldest daughter across the face.

William quickly moved to place himself between his wife and her mother. Over his shoulder, William shouted. "How dare you? Madam, I now warn you, never strike my wife again."

These words caused silence to overtake the room, an eerie silence which was unheard of at Longbourn.

Mr Gardiner looked between the other men and his niece. Gerald decided to speak, praying his son would not strike his mother in law.

"It seems that our two families met as they were all attempting to escape Vienna. Your niece and nephew were boarding the ship that they were going to take, on the Danube, in hopes of escaping the invading army. Unfortunately, a bullet struck you nephew, and he was killed. His body fell into the river, nearly taking Elizabeth with him. This is my son, Fitzwilliam. He was there, with Lady Matlock and her son. The young men saved Elizabeth from toppling into the water. She has been with them ever since. And they married just before returning to England, with my sister in law's blessing."

"Uncle, why are you here, at Longbourn?" Elizabeth asked. There was a red mark on her cheek, where her mother had struck her.

"Lizzy, perhaps it would be best if you took a seat. I see there is much about which we all need to speak." Mr Gardiner stated, motioning towards the sofa that would allow William and Elizabeth to sit together. "Lizzy, your aunt is here as well, though she and Mary went to Meryton to see your Aunt Phillips."

As the couple moved towards the sofa, Mrs Bennet was furious. "If Alex is not here, then I want her out of my home. It is still my home, even though Mr Bennet's cousin has informed us he will take possession immediately."

Those words struck horror in Elizabeth's heart. "There would be no need for Papa's cousin to come immediately. Papa does not require his assistance."

"Lizzy, please, take a seat." Mr Gardiner stated softly.

Jane knew her sister would suffer significantly. "Lizzy, it would be best to sit on the sofa. Please."

"NO...NO...Papa, Papa..." Elizabeth began to break free from her husband and head for the door. She would go to his study, where he preferred to be, reading a book. Before she could reach the parlor door, Mr Gardiner had taken ahold of her by the arm.

"Lizzy, my dear girl, your father..."

That was the last Elizabeth heard, as her world turned black and she collapsed.

~~~~~~~ ** ~~~~~~~

Chapter 11

Before opening her eyes, Elizabeth knew her husband was sitting beside her, lightly caressing the back of her hand. This had become his way of showing her his support, without words.

She was lying down, but she was not certain where she was. That is, until she opened her eyes. Seeing that they were in her bedchambers at Longbourn, it took a moment to comprehend why she would be there, with William at her side. Then the world came crashing down on her, and the pain grew in intensity.

"Papa, he is..."

William looked her in the eyes, and the sorrow he felt for her was plain to see. "Yes, my dearest. I wish it were not true. From what your uncle stated, when your father learned of the invasion, he collapsed from an attack of apoplexy. He was to suffer three more attacks in the space of a week. Your father finally found peace four days ago."

"Poor Papa. He believed us both dead. How I wish I could have arrived before his... just to see him one last time."

"I wish the same, my love. It pains me that you have had such tragedy befall your family. My father is speaking with your uncle at the moment. It appears that your father's cousin, Mr Collins, had planned to come here, in search of a wife from you and your sisters. He wished to have a connection with your family, to mend the breech which had happened when your father and his argued many years ago. Mr Collins felt that giving one of your sisters a secure home and life, he would be doing your father a great service. He arrived just two days after the news and Mr Bennet's collapse. The man is a clergyman, with a living in Kent. When he heard the news of you and Alex missing, potentially dead, and your father's condition, the greedy toad decided to stay in the neighborhood. Due to his constant surveying of the property with his greedy eyes, and estimating how long until he could take over the house. When Mr Gardiner arrived, Mr Collins was moved to the dower house."

"And now, he will inherit everything?" Elizabeth asked, already knowing the answer.

William nodded his head. "And, from what I have been told, the toad feels he deserves to marry your elder sister."

Elizabeth sat straight up. "Jane? He feels he deserves to marry my Jane? From what you have said, and what Papa has said over the years, Mr Collins is a horrible person. I could not endure seeing my sister forced into such a marriage. But what are we to do to protect her?"

"Father is speaking with Mr Gardiner. They will find the best solution for everything, have no fear. Perhaps we will purchase a cottage in which your mother and sisters can live. Or they can stay with relations. I am far more concerned with you at the moment. You collapsed, and I was certain some illness had taken hold of you. Fortunately, I was close enough to catch you, so you did not harm yourself."

"I wish to speak with my uncle. Can we join him and your father?"

"Elizabeth, I think it would be wisest for you to rest further. After all you have been through, you have not rested or eaten as you should have. Mrs Hill is having some tea and biscuits sent up for you."

"My father, I cannot believe he is gone. And he died believing I was dead. It is my fault, as I told Alex I envied his going on such a holiday. I have always wished to see the world; see places I have only read described. Alex spoke to Papa on my behalf, convincing him of the wonderful opportunity I would have by going with my brother. Now they are both gone, and Mamma despises me. I wish I had never gone on the journey." Elizabeth turned to her side, her back to her husband, as she began to sob anew.

"As much as I wish you had remained here and not having your life in danger as it was throughout the ordeal, I would not have met you, and you would not be my beloved wife." William ran his fingers over her back, gently massaging her tight muscles, caused from all the pain and grief she had suffered.

"I will only bring you shame, William. You deserve so much more than my ruining your life. Perhaps, if you applied for annulment, you can be released from this wretched situation."

William's hand held still. "Is that your wish? Do you desire to be rid of me?"

"Of course not. I am thinking of you. My family is in a terrible situation and it would be selfish of me to force you into such a mess. I love you, and want the best for you."

"You are the best for me, Elizabeth. Believe me, you are the very best part of my life." William leaned over his wife, placing a chaste kiss on her lips. "Now, I insist you remain here and rest. Father and I are planning to speak with Mr Gardiner, before we all speak with this Collins person. It appears that your uncle, Mr Phillips, has gone to Town to learn of the disposition of the estate. According to what Mr Phillips stated, the entailment was broken with your brother's birth. Mr Collins seems to believe he is the rightful heir, as there are no other males in the Bennet family. While Father and you uncle discuss the matter, I wish for you to rest. Your sister informed me she would be pleased to spend time with you while I meet with the other men."

"I would love to have some time with Jane. I want to know all there is to be known of the time since Alex and I left for Vienna." Elizabeth gave her husband a slight grin as she agreed with her husband.

"I love you, Elizabeth. Do not ever forget how dearly I love you."

"I demand you remove that...that...good for nothing girl from my home. Until Mr Collins throws me to the hedgerow, this is my home, and I refuse to have her staying here. Remove her immediately." Fanny Bennet was livid. She wished to be rid of her most troublesome daughter, especially since she felt the deaths of Mr Bennet and Alex rested solely on Elizabeth's shoulders.

"Sister, calm yourself. We need to discuss all that we now know has happened. If you allow us, we shall be able to know what will happen to you and my nieces." Mr Gardiner attempted to appease his sister.

"I will not allow her to stay here, even for an hour. She is the cause of all our woes, and I will not tolerate her being here." Mrs Bennet's hand was in constant motion, waving a handkerchief as added influence. "For years, I have tried to prove to my husband that she was the devil and would bring us nothing but misery. Now she arrives here, after killing her brother and causing the death of her father, with a man she claims to have married. You will not take what little I have to care for my remaining daughters. She deserves no such blessings from me."

"Then allow me to ease your fears in that direction. Mr Darcy and his son are very wealthy. They have the largest estate in Derbyshire, and more than enough to see to Elizabeth's needs. If you were to be kind to your daughter and her husband, they could even be a blessing to you and the other girls."

"I want nothing from the likes of them. Most likely there would be a curse attached to anything they were to give us. Only the worst sort would wish to be connected with that chit. No, I wash my hands of her, and good riddance. My Jane will marry well, and take care of me. Perhaps we can arrange for her to marry Mr Collins. Then I would never have to leave Longbourn." Mrs Bennet's eyes lit with such a thought.

"After meeting Thomas' cousin, I would never allow such a union." Mr Gardiner declared. "My nieces deserve far better than that sycophantic toad."

Mrs Bennet ignored her brother, as she continued her plotting to arrange a marriage which would give her the security she desired.

A knock was heard on the door of the study, and Mrs Phillips, Mrs Bennet's sister, entered the room. "Fanny, I just spoke with Mr Darcy and his son. They are willing to purchase a cottage for you and the girls, and provide an allowance for your upkeep. You would never have to worry again. It is quite generous, and they would set up dowries for Jane, Mary, Kitty, and Lydia."

"We will not need their blood money. Jane shall marry Mr Collins, and we will remain here, at Longbourn." Fanny held her chin high as she spoke.

Appalled, Mr Gardiner decided it was time to put his foot down. He was the head of the Gardiner family, which included his sister and her children. "Sister, I will not hear you speak such nonsense. Your son in law and his father have brought us a wonderful option, one that will give your unmarried daughters a chance for felicitous marriages. How could you not wish for such for them?"

"I could not live in a house paid for with their money. It would be tainted." Mrs Bennet stated, her arms crossed across her chest.

"Then you will have to find somewhere to live on your own." Mr Gardiner announced. "Your daughters will be under my protection, and I will not allow you to force them to marry the likes of Mr Collins. If necessary, I will take the girls with me to Town. They will find the lives they deserve, not something you design for them."

Mrs Bennet stood and marched to her brother, standing toe to toe with him. "You have no right to make decisions for my daughters. I am their mother; it is my decision that will be considered."

Mrs Phillips was certain her husband would return soon, and all of this would be unnecessary. "My husband will learn the truth of the entailment, and what impact Alex's death will have. Our brother is thinking of what is best for your family, as he is the head of our family."

"I beg to differ, Mrs Phillips." A sniveling voice came from the doorway. Turning, the trio spied Mr William Collins. "As their father's heir, I believe that I have say over an uncle on their mother's side of the family. And I wish to support my dear cousin's widow in her decision. She is their mother, and wishes only the best for her offspring. A more devoted mother you would never find."

"Mr Collins, this conversation does not have anything to do with you." Mrs Phillips stated. "Mr Gardiner, as the head of the Gardiner family, does have rights over his sister. Just wait until my husband returns. I am certain you will find you have no say in the matter."

"Ah, but her daughters are Bennets, and I am the head of the Bennet family. I was informed that Miss Elizabeth has returned, though sadly, Master Alex did not. I believe that makes me the head of the family, therefore, it is up to me to decide their futures."

"Mr Collins, I will not allow you to take advantage of the situation. I am well aware of your desire to marry one of my nieces. It is my duty to protect them from such a situation." Mr Gardiner stated.

"Forgive me, Mr Gardiner, but I want what is best for my relations. If that includes one of the fine young ladies becoming my wife, it will only make us closer as a family. Mrs Bennet is a loving mother, and it is only right for her to wish the best for her children. She has five daughters, and the ones I have seen are quite beautiful. If the last one is even half as pretty as her sisters, she will be a perfect bride for me."

Mr Gardiner looked at the former parson in

disgust. "Mr Collins, my niece, Elizabeth, is married. She married before returning to England."

"That cannot be. She did not have the permission of her father or guardian, and, if I am not mistaken, Miss Elizabeth is not of age to wed without permission. Therefore, the marriage could not be legal."

"My niece was married in another country. She did not require the approval of her guardian to make such a decision. You must be familiar with people crossing the border to Scotland, so they can marry before they are of age and without parental consent." Mr Gardiner said, his nerves were nearly frazzled from having to contend with the slimy man for days on end.

Mr Collins was not easily dissuaded. "I am certain that the formality of an annulment will be easily attained. Who is the man in question? He was most likely lured by my cousin's beauty and now realizes he does not wish to be married to her. What is the name of this man, so I might speak with him?"

"His name is Fitzwilliam Darcy of Pemberley." Mr Gardiner announced. "He is here, with his father, with Elizabeth."

"Mr Darcy? Is he not the nephew of Lady Catherine de Bourgh of Rosings Park? My patroness speaks often of her nephew. But he cannot be married to my cousin, for Lady Catherine has told me many times that Mr Fitzwilliam Darcy is engaged to her daughter, Miss Anne de Bourgh. Mr Darcy is most likely desirous of an annulment. It has long been the expectations of their family that Master Fitzwilliam Darcy would marry his cousin. And someone will require taking Cousin Elizabeth as their wife, to keep the respectability of the family. I am more than willing to marry my cousin."

Mrs Phillips was growing more and more suspicious. With there being five sisters, and Elizabeth had not been seen by this man, why was he adamant to marry her?

"Mrs Bennet stated that she wished for you to marry my niece Jane. Why would you determine you wish to marry Elizabeth, when you have never met the young lady? I admit, my niece is beautiful, but that cannot be the reason. All of my nieces are beautiful." Mrs Phillips inquired.

"Well...I...have heard of Cousin Elizabeth's attributes. It is my opinion that she would please me better than the other sisters."

"Mr Collins, Lizzy is not near as beautiful as my

Jane. Jane's features are delicate, which is popular to the upper circles, from what I have read. Her blonde hair, blue eyes, slim figure, all are what young men desire." Fanny Bennet wished for one of her other daughters to become the next Mistress, as they would be easier to manipulate.

Mr Gardiner noted that Mr Collins was nervous about the conversation. Then it became obvious to the uncle. Besides Jane, Mary and the twins were fair haired. And, like the women on their father's side of the family, they were very...lacking in curves. Of all the sisters, Elizabeth was endowed with the sort of curves, like her mother, that men prefer. And Elizabeth was also the one with the dark colored hair. Obviously, the man had heard about Elizabeth, and decided she was more to his liking.

"Mr Collins, if you would allow me a moment, I will fetch Mr Darcy and his son. I believe it is important for them to be a part of this conversation." Mr Gardiner said, as he made his way towards the door.

"There is no need for them to be involved in our family matters." Mr Collins decided. He was not willing to cause any difficulties for his patroness' family. "It will suffice that we inform them that we are willing to grant the annulment, releasing the young man, so he can fulfill his family's greatest duty."

"I believe it is best that the two gentlemen join us, Mr Collins." Mrs Phillips concurred with her brother.

~~~~~~~ ** ~~~~~~~

Chapter 12

Mr Darcy and William entered the room, following Mr Gardiner. The men looked about, finding Mr Collins standing beside Mrs Bennet, as he spoke reassuringly to her.

"Have no fear, Mrs Bennet. I will see that all is managed the way we wish. As the head of the Bennet family, I promise you that an annulment will be obtained and the foolishness of this will be behind us. Once I am wed, all will be well."

"What is this discussion of an annulment?" Mr Darcy asked, his brows meeting as the crease between them grew. "You cannot be referring to my son's marriage to Elizabeth. It is legal and binding."

"Ah, my good sir, we have yet to meet."

"And as you are the lower ranking person in the room, I feel it is my place to inform you that approaching me is improper. But I do remember you, Mr Collins. I have been the advisor to my wife's sister, Lady Catherine de Bourgh. I remember seeing you from across a field, and grateful I was so far from you. Now, what is going on here? My son and his wife wish to rest, for they have been on a long and difficult journey."

"As I was saying, as Lady Catherine's spiritual advisor, I feel honor bound to remind you of your son's duty to his cousin. Miss Anne has been waiting for you to finally arrive and marry her." Mr Collins puffed out his chest, so proud was he to be given such an honor.

Mr Darcy was appalled. "Mr Collins, you have no knowledge of what is to happen in our family. My wife did not, and I repeat myself, not, plan an arrangement for Anne and William to marry. It is none of your business, who my son marries. Lady Catherine has no control over William's choice of bride, and I demand you mind your own business."

"But Sir...Miss Anne will be devastated to learn of her betrothed spurning her. Your family will disapprove. The Earl and Countess, they will never approve of such a low born female becoming a member of your family." Mr Collins was grasping at any possible reason for the marriage to be dissolved. Lady Catherine had spoken so often of the union between her daughter and her nephew, and Collins knew he did not wish to have the grand dame angry at himself, for Elizabeth was his cousin. And the man had caught a glimpse of his cousin.

The Bennet girls were pretty, yet they lacked the sort of figure that he preferred. And he preferred dark hair to light. Seeing the second eldest daughter, the way she filled out her gown, Collins was certain that none of the other sisters could compare. William Collins was determined, he deserved Elizabeth Bennet.

He was brought from his woolgathering by the voice of the younger Darcy.

"Mr Collins, as my father has informed you, Lady Catherine does not have any claim on what I do with my life. I made the decision to marry a young lady with whom I have fallen in love, and we married on the continent. That is the end of the discussion. There is not going to be an annulment, do I make myself clear?"

"But...but...her Ladyship...she will be terribly upset. You must take into consideration such superior breeding, Miss de Bourgh is far better suited..."

William walked up to the blundering fool and took hold of the toad's lapel. "This is the final word on the matter. I will not be seeking an annulment. Elizabeth is my wife, and will remain my wife. That is all there is to the matter."

Stepping back, as William released the parson, Mr

Collins turned his attention towards Mrs Bennet. "Madame, you had stated I was within my rights to choose from your five daughters. You have deceived me, and therefore, I resend my offer to make one of your daughters my wife. Thus, you will need to remove yourself from my home immediately."

Mrs Bennet's wailing could be heard throughout the house. "This cannot be...we are ruined...that foolish chit, she has ruined everything. She is no longer my daughter. I refuse to claim her as my daughter. Never again will she be welcome wherever I am. My other girls, oh the poor dears, they will never be able to find good matches, due to Lizzy's selfishness. It is not to be borne."

"Sister, you are a fool. Why do you turn your back on the generous offer you have before you?" Mr Gardiner was shocked at his sister's behavior. "You are cutting off your nose to spite your face. Mr Darcy is offering you a home of your own."

"A small cottage, why would I wish a small cottage, when I could have this home for the rest of my life?"

"Fanny, do you honestly believe that you would be the Mistress of Longbourn, if one of your daughters were married to Mr Collins?" Mrs Phillips asked. "You would be the dower, and your daughter would be the Mistress."

"My daughters all know that my opinions are superior to their own, therefore, I would remain the Mistress of Longbourn. My daughter will need to step back and watch me as I show her the duties of the Mistress of this estate." Mrs Bennet puffed up her chest and stood tall in her pride.

"No, Mamma, I would not allow you to be in charge of my home, no matter who I married." Elizabeth had heard her mother's cries and came downstairs to have her say in the matter. "Father knew that his cousin was a fool, he told me, before I left with Alex. He would never approve of my marrying such a man, especially since I have a husband who loves and respects me. I will never consent to having my marriage annulled."

Mrs Bennet was angrier than she had ever been. If it had been possible, puffs of steam would shoot out of her ears and nostrils. Before anyone knew what was happening, Mrs Bennet grabbed a handful of her daughter's hair, yanking on the bun, dislodging the pins. She began smacking her daughter's face, all the while she was screaming insults at Elizabeth.

Mr Darcy and Mr Gardiner grabbed hold of Mrs Bennet, as she continued reaching for her daughter. Mr Collins managed to place himself between the mother and daughter, his hand slipping into a most inappropriate position of the daughter's bosom.

Before he had a chance to do any further assault on her body, William and his father were able to pull her free of the scoundrel.

"Mr Collins, it is difficult for me to believe you to be a man of the cloth." Mr Darcy spat the words at the man. "Do not think, for one moment, that I did not witness what you just did. The liberties you just forced upon my daughter is grounds to be called out. You are no gentleman, nor should you be a clergyman. I will be contacting my cousin, the Archbishop of Canterbury. He will be very displeased with your actions."

"I have no notion of what you are speaking." Mr Collins stated. "I have done nothing improper."

"You fondled my wife's person, Mr Collins." William hissed.

"As a man of the cloth, I would never do such a vulgar act. Besides, you should never have married. I was promised my choice of brides from the Bennet sisters. From what I had been told, it was Miss Elizabeth I decided would meet my needs."

"Fit your needs?" Mrs Phillips was having difficulty keeping from snarling. "I learned from Sir William Lucas the sort of questions with which you plagued him, at the dinner three nights ago. Sir William's son, Robert, told me of the questions you asked, regarding my niece's figure. No decent man would ever speak of a gentlewoman in such terms. Robert was shocked at your words, Mr Collins. When he informed his father, Sir William sent the young man to me and warned me of what you were saying."

Fitzwilliam Darcy turned towards Mrs Phillips. "What did this man say of my wife's figure." Each word was said as the gentleman attempted to keep his hands from strangling Collins.

"I...I...simply asked...which of my cousins had the most pleasing figure. As I had yet to meet Miss Elizabeth, I wished to determine if I should wait, to see if she returned. And of course, it would not have mattered, had her brother returned with her."

"You asked if my niece's breasts were firm and sizeable." Mrs Phillips said, unable to believe that Collins had dared to lie so completely.

William needed no further enticement to deal with the pompous clergyman. Mr Collins was laid out on the floor with a single blow. Mrs Bennet was screaming, deafening them with her tirade. She was defending Mr Collins, calling William names that shocked even her siblings. When she broke free from her brothers, Mrs Bennet flung herself to the floor, sobbing for Mr Collins to wake.

Mr Darcy turned his attention to his son. "William,

perhaps you should take Elizabeth upstairs."

"I want that chit out of my home." Mrs Bennet screeched, as she half laid on the floor, holding one of Collins' hands to her cheek. "I want all of you out of my home. Mr Collins requires peace and calm; I will not allow you to overwhelm him any further."

Elizabeth and William made their way from the room, just as Mrs Hill was bringing a pitcher of cold water for those remaining. William could not help but smile when he turned his head and witnessed his father dumping the contents of the pitcher over the unconscious form of Mr Collins. Mrs Hill was shaking as she left the room, the pitcher having been restored to her hands. Once she was a safe distance from the room, the housekeeper began laughing, until her sides began to ache.

~~ ** ~~

The decision was made that the Darcy family would stay at the inn in Meryton, so a message was sent to secure the necessary rooms they would require.

While the Darcys were still at Longbourn, the reunion with her family gave Elizabeth strength. Jane was pleased to have her dearest sister nearby, though she missed the bond they once had. With Elizabeth married, her first priority was to her husband.

Mrs Gardiner had returned to Longbourn, thrilled to see her niece had returned. "Oh Lizzy, we feared the worst. We have been given a great gift with your return."

"But Alex did not survive, Aunt Helen."

"And your brother would be grateful for your survival. He loved you dearly, and would not wish for you to have died." Mrs Gardiner spoke in a soothing voice. She held her niece close to her. "We are so relieved that you are well. And married. What a surprise."

Mr Darcy smiled. "Who would have thought that our relations would return to us together, not to mention married? When your husband met with Lord Matlock and myself, there was not a thought of them being together. It was shocking when we first met Elizabeth and realized who she was."

"I am pleased that he spoke of the situation with Lizzy and Alex. You were able to assist in returning Lizzy here. This has guaranteed you a special place in the hearts of our family."

"Your husband informed me that you are from Lambton." Mr Darcy stated. "How long ago did you leave there?"

"I lived there until I was seventeen. My mother's

aunt was ill and I went to stay with her as a companion. One day, I went to purchase some fabric from a warehouse, and I met Edward. He was working at the warehouse and was the clerk who assisted me."

"And your family, are they still in Lambton?"

"No, my father died five years past, and my mother lives with a cousin in a village ten miles from Town."

"My aunt has always spoken of the beauty of Derbyshire." Elizabeth announced. "I must admit, I am excited to see my new home."

"Lizzy will be finding her way around all of the trails within the first month. She is notorious for her long walks in nature." Mrs Gardiner chuckled.

"Well, my dear daughter, you will be forced to wait until after everything is resolved here." Mr Darcy advised. "It may take some time before we can leave."

Elizabeth's face dipped downward. For a moment, she had forgotten the reason they were all in Hertfordshire.

"If you are to remain in the area, you will most likely wish to have somewhere to stay rather than at the inn. Though it is comfortable, you might wish for somewhere else to stay." Mrs Phillips added to the conversation. "My husband holds the ability of leasing out Netherfield Park, which is the next estate over. It is larger than Longbourn, but it will allow you the comforts to which you are accustomed. We would have no problem in staffing the house."

Mr Darcy looked at his son. He knew his son wished for some time with his bride, and he knew that Elizabeth was worn from all the upheaval in her life. It would be good for her to have some time to adjust, in relatively familiar surroundings. They could lease Netherfield for a month, which would allow his new daughter to make a farewell to her former life, and become comfortable with her new role in life. It would allow them to determine the living arrangements for the remainder of the Bennet family. Mr Darcy thought of sending for his Georgiana to join them. She was currently staying at Pemberley with her governess.

"The more I think of your suggestion, the more I like the idea. Shall we lease for a month with the option of extending, if there be a need?"

Mrs Phillips nodded her head. "I know my husband will approve of your leasing Netherfield, so the paperwork can be done when he returns. There is a housekeeper, a butler, a cook and one maid who live there all of the time. Mrs Norton is very capable and can have staff hired by morning. I will send word to her to prepare for your arrival, she should be able to prepare a few rooms for your use tonight, then more tomorrow. And we can send word to the inn that you will not be requiring the rooms."

"Please take this payment for the inn." Mr Darcy reached into his pocket and drew out some coins. "I do not wish to see them lose the income they expected from us."

"Very kind, Mr Darcy. I know they will appreciate your generosity." Mrs Phillips made her way to write the messages, then went to the stable to have the young hand deliver them.

~~ ** ~~

Mr Collins was unbearable when he became conscious. The cold water shook him, and he came off the floor, sputtering. "What is going on here? Where is Miss Elizabeth?"

"Mrs Darcy is with her husband and his father." Mr Gardiner responded. "We are making arrangements to have my nieces removed from this estate, and I ask you to give us a few more days to find the best situation for them."

"They are my relations, and it is up to me to determine what is best for them. As I have been denied the daughter I wished to make my wife, I am extremely displeased. I will not allow you to remove any of the other sisters. My authority over my relations, as head of the Bennet family, gives me the right to make the decisions for their future."

"Our nieces are closer in relationship to us than they are to you, as you are only a distant cousin. You may have inherited the estate, but you did not inherit the young ladies. Do what you will with my sister, but my nieces will be with us." Mr Gardiner declared.

"I believe you are incorrect. Perhaps you should check with your other brother in law, as I believe I will be found correct. Legally, you have no standing. It is my decision to make as to where they will reside." Mr Collins was filled with anger. "And I demand you leave my home immediately. Take all of your other relations from my lands, and do not return. The Bennets will remain here, with me. I will not tolerate any contact with them. Do I make myself clear?"

"Mr Collins, I would never leave my nieces in your home. Never. The girls will be coming with me. We will have them packed and out of here as soon as possible."

"I demand you leave my home immediately. If you remove anything or anyone from my property, I will send for the magistrate to deal with you." Collins shouted. "Until I am told by the magistrate that I have no right to protect my cousins, they will remain with me."

Mrs Phillips was at a loss as to what to do. The papers that Thomas Bennet signed left the estate to Alex. The entailment was dissolved with Alex's birth, and no plans had been put in place for Alex's death. Technically, Mr Collins had no real claim to the estate, though he would have to obtain a ruling from the magistrate to determine the estate's true owner. But Mr Phillips was uncertain as to whether the estate would be transferred to Jane, being the eldest daughter, or if it would revert to the crown to be gifted to another, so he had made the journey to Town to discuss the matter with some of the best legal minds he knew.

"Mr Collins, perhaps it would be best if we send to Lucas Lodge, and ask Sir William Lucas to come. With Mr Bennet's death, Sir William became the magistrate. It would be wise for us to clear some matters."

Mr Collins was leery. He did not wish to have anyone closely examine his claim. "There is no need to waste the man's time. The estate has been handed down through the male line of the Bennet family. My father told me that if Thomas did not have an heir, I would become the heir. No female member of the family can inherit. Therefore, I am the head of the Bennet family."

"Until my husband returns with further information, Sir William Lucas has the authority to make decisions, such as whether you can keep my nieces against their will. If you are unwilling to allow Sir William to render a decision, then I suggest you try to throw us from this estate. But remember, the staff of Longbourn are loyal to the Bennet family, not the Collins family. Most of the servants have known my nieces since the girls were babes. Who do you think they will defend?"

Mr Gardiner was proud of his sister, the manner in which she was able to stand up to the clergyman. *And for years, I believed her to be as silly as Fanny. She is nothing like our sister.*

Mr Collins was furious. "Then take the chits and be gone. But they cannot remove anything from the estate, no even a ribbon or a button. Do you hear me? They leave with the gowns on their backs."

"It is not proven to be your inheritance, Mr Collins. By refusing to allow the girls to take their personal belongings, you are doing yourself no favor in the eyes of the law." Mrs Phillips stated. "Would you prefer to be seen as a man who treated his cousins abombibly or that you have a Christian heart?"

The man scowled at the intelligent woman. "They may take one satchel each. And make them hurry, as I wish to be alone."

"But...but...Mr Collins, I cannot leave Longbourn." Mrs Bennet cried. "You would not toss me to the hedgerow, would you?"

"After all the promises that have been broken, you are fortunate I have not demanded your removal immediately." Mr Collins glared at the woman. "But I will allow you to remain here, for the time being. I see that you are a victim of your second daughter, as much as I have become."

Fanny Bennet preened as she looked at the others in the room. "I will make amends, Mr Collins. I promise you, you will not regret your decision."

~~~~~~~ ** ~~~~~~~

Chapter 13

Jane, Mary, Kitty and Lydia quickly gathered their most prize possessions and stuffed them in satchels and trunks. In a matter of minutes, they had all they could grab and were downstairs, prepared to leave their home. Elizabeth had also gone to what had been her bedchambers, gathering her belongings. William was on hand to assist her, and they made quick work of the task.

The girls were loaded in the Gardiner carriage, with their aunts and uncle. The Darcys climbed in their carriage, which was to follow the other to Netherfield. The entire family party would remain at Netherfield, together, including Mrs Phillips. She decided she would prefer being with her relations than alone at her home.

As the carriages came to a halt in front of Netherfield, Mrs Norton and Mr Burke, the butler, came outside. "My goodness, Mrs Phillips, you were not exaggerating. You brought quite a party to our door."

"Forgive me, Mrs Norton, I believe it is safer that

we brought everyone here for the time being. The girls can share rooms, Jane and Mary in one and the twins in another. And Lizzy, she is now a married woman. This is her husband, Mr Fitzwilliam Darcy, and his father." Mrs Phillips was well known to the housekeeper. "We will make do for tonight, then hire more staff tomorrow."

"And I can send to our townhouse, requesting some of our servants come." Mr Darcy stated. "I can send one of my men tonight, and they will be here tomorrow."

"That would be wonderful, Mr Darcy." Mr Gardiner said. "Would it be possible to have our nanny bring our children here? I do not believe this situation will be corrected anytime soon. We may be forced to stay in the neighborhood for a fortnight."

"Write down the information and I will have my postilion take a message to your home. We have two carriages and a wagon in town, so there should be plenty of room."

~~ ** ~~

The following day brought sunlight and smiles, as Elizabeth woke with her family, old and new. Waking up in her husband's arms brought great comfort to her, and Elizabeth thanked God for his blessing.

"I do not know what I have done to deserve your love, William, but I am grateful." Elizabeth whispered as she lay resting her head on his chest.

"It is I who does not deserve such a gift as your love, but I refuse to ever allow you to get away from me." William placed a gentle kiss on the top of her head. "You are so dear to me, and I promise to cherish you as the gift that God sent to me."

"Can you ever forgive me for my family's behavior? It was insanity, Mamma and Mr Collins."

"My dearest love, your mother and Collins are out of their minds. Your mother is understandable, as she is living with fear. With your father and brother dead, she is terrified as to the future. And the fear makes her lash out at you. She wishes her life to return to what it was, with the security she felt."

"You are too kind, William. Too kind indeed. My mother is a foolish woman, and you make excuses for her behavior."

"For you, I will forgive your mother. But the cousin..."

"I have no understanding of that man. He is ridiculous." Elizabeth was still shocked at the clergyman's behavior.

"Well, let us rise for the day. Once we are dressed, we can break our fast, and determine what we will do today." William suggested.

Elizabeth nodded in agreement. The two remained in their embrace, neither wishing to be the one to initiate movement which would pull them apart.

~~ ** ~~

When Elizabeth and William arrived in the dining room, they found the room filled with their relations. Mr and Mrs Gardiner were speaking with Elizabeth's sisters, and Mr Darcy was listening to Mrs Phillips ramble on about her husband's profession.

"My husband will be able to determine the rights of my nieces. I am certain he will return in the next day or two. Mr Phillips is quite intelligent and a well-respected solicitor."

"I have no doubt. Elizabeth spoke of you and your husband, and the Gardiners, on our way from Town. She loves and respects you very much." Mr Darcy confessed. "Without the support of your family, I do not know what would have happened last night."

"I must admit, I was nervous at first, but then I saw how foolish my sister was being, and what she was putting in jeopardy, to have things her way, and I saw red. I could not stay silent, not when my nieces were put in such a position. My husband will be surprised when he learns what I did."

Mr Darcy chuckled. "I will make sure to compliment your intelligence and quick mind in rescuing the young ladies."

"Hopefully, he will return in the next day or two. I honestly miss him."

Mr Gardiner turned his attention to his sister. "I sent a message to your husband, my dear sister. Since he is staying in our home while he is in Town, he will know what is going on when the message is delivered for our children and their nanny to make the journey to join us."

"Let us pray that he will soon have the answer for which he is searching. I do not wish to see the girls robbed of their futures." Mrs Phillips wiped a tear that had pooled in the corner of her eye.

"Have no fear, Sister. We will see them protected."

~~ ** ~~

"Mrs Bennet, what are we to do? You knew the entail was broken, and now, everyone else knows. What will happen to my claim for the estate?" Mr Collins paced about the parlor.

"If only Mr Phillips had not been here. Why could he not have been away when this all happened? Once we had you married to Jane, everything would have been perfect."

"I would have preferred Miss Elizabeth. Your other daughters do not have figures that would tempt me nearly as much as does Miss Elizabeth's."

"Is it my fault that you are thinking of your preferences for the marital bed, and not of the security of the estate." Mrs Bennet said with a hint of distaste. "Had you accepted Jane, everything could have been accomplished quickly and without difficulty. But no, you insisted you must wait to see if Lizzy was still alive. Why is it that men do not think rationally when it comes to the woman they are to bed? You can always take a mistress after you are married. You do not have to like your wife's figure to make the relationship work."

"My belief is that one should not have to pay for something he could get for free if he chooses the bride that will suit him." Mr Collins huffed.

"Jane is not without a bosom, why could you not find her preferable?"

"Madame, your eldest daughter is not much larger than a schoolboy. I wish to have a woman in my bed in which I can take pleasure."

"Well, I cannot see that you will ever know Lizzy's figure, as that Darcy boy seems to be completely enthralled with her."

Mr Collins growled. "I cannot believe that my misfortune is his pleasure. He is wealthy, heir to one of the largest estates in Derbyshire. And he was to marry Miss Anne de Bourgh, who is an heiress. It is simply not fair. He could have any lady he wished, and a dozen mistresses, yet he chooses your second born daughter."

"There is nothing to be done about it now, Mr Collins. You will need to decide whether or not to accept the situation and marry Jane, or find some other young lady. But you should keep in mind, I will not be forced to leave my home. I have assisted you every step, and will not be dislodged due to Lizzy not being available for you to marry."

"I should have you tossed from the house this very moment." Mr Collins was aggravated beyond rational thought. "You have been unable to secure any of the promises you made to me. You were certain that your daughter was alive, though were certain your son was not. How did you come to such an understanding of the status of your children?"

"As a mother, I can feel each of my children in my soul. I was certain that something had happened to

Alex, and after we received word of the French army attacking Vienna, I knew he had been killed. With Lizzy, well, there was an emptiness, but there was still something telling me that she was alive."

"You are such a remarkable mother, Mrs Bennet." Mr Collins declared sarcastically.

"I am practical, Mr Collins. My children can fend for themselves. What am I to do? How am I to live? No one will take care of my comfort, so it is left to me to arrange."

"Why would you have refused the offer of Mr Darcy, for him to purchase a cottage for you?"

"And be at the mercy of a man who is unknown to me? A cottage... some small residence in which I will be forced to remain for the rest of my life. No, I will not be reduced to such a degradation, when I should have this home for the remainder of my years."

"You passed on an opportunity to use your whiles on Mr Darcy. He is a widower, and you could have forced a compromise to make him marry you. His estate would make Longbourn appear to be a small cottage. From what Lady Catherine has told me, there are more than five and twenty bedchambers alone at Pemberley. It is huge, and you could have been the Mistress of that estate." Mr Collins wished to be rid of the woman he had pledged to protect, a pledge he had made in an effort to secure his late cousin's estate.

"I prefer to remain here. Everyone knows me. Why would I wish to start all over? And a man such as Mr Darcy is not as compliant to his wife's wishes as was Mr Bennet. My late husband was agreeable to most anything I decided, just so he could keep the peace in our home."

"Well, you will need to control your behavior, so we both benefit from our arrangement. I sent off word to my patroness, Lady Catherine. She will make certain that your daughter's marriage is annulled, as she has long desired a marriage between the younger Mr Darcy and her daughter."

"What good will that do for us? It is clear that Lizzy will not marry you, and is most likely carrying a child by that man. A bastard child will do nothing but add to our problems. You must marry Jane, as soon as possible. Purchase a special license, so you can marry quickly."

"When your daughter is disgraced from an annulment, she will need someone to make her legitimate once again. And I will be very willing to have her as my wife."

Mrs Bennet huffed. "Lizzy stated she would not allow me to remain here, as I am."

"Have no fear, Mrs Bennet. Your daughter will learn to tolerate your remaining as the Mistress of Longbourn, even if she requires my teaching her some...lessons." Mr Collins' statement was clear, as his right hand, fisted tight, struck his left palm.

~~ ** ~~

Mrs Hill was devoted to the Bennet family, with one exception. That exception was Mrs Bennet. While she tolerated the wife of her master, who was the mother of the six children that Mrs Hill loved, there was something about Fanny Bennet that set her housekeeper against her. Perhaps it was the way Mrs Bennet had always treated Elizabeth.

Fanny Bennet was pleased to have her son and the required heir as her first born. The pressure to give her husband an heir was relieved, and allowed the nervous wife to calm. Her next child being a daughter was no worry either. But then a second daughter was born. In Mrs Bennet's way of thinking, Elizabeth had been a disappointment. There was always room for a a spare to the heir, and Elizabeth should have been the spare. Once Mrs Bennet had been overheard speaking with Mrs Long of her agitation over Elizabeth not being a son. Mrs Hill was appalled, never having been blessed with children in all her ten years of marriage. So a child, no matter boy or girl, was viewed as a precious gift. While the mother bemoaned of having a second daughter, the housekeeper decided to always be a motherly figure to the girl. And she would protect Elizabeth from her mother.

Having overheard Mrs Bennet and the odius Mr Collings speaking, Mrs Hill decided to do what she could to protect the Bennet daughters. The week before Mr Bennet was stricken with apoplexy, he had called his housekeeper and Butler into his study. Mrs Hill could remember the conversation clearly.

"I wished to speak to you on an important matter." Mrs Bennet stated. "I have just spoken with Mr Jones, the apothecary, and feel that I need to take you into my confidence. Had my brother in law, Mr Phillips, been available, there would be no need for me to do this, but he is contending with his uncle's situation at the moment, and I am sure that there will be no need to make him return to the neighborhood so quickly."

"My cousin, a Mr Collins, is to arrive. If he is anything like his father, he is a fool and pompous as the day is long. I wish to have you be aware, as the father was furious when Fanny gave birth to Alex. With the entail broken, the Collins line does not stand a chance to inherit. But I worry, as Anthony, the father, long believed that they should have some part of the inheritance. The son might take advantage of his visit."

"Should we lock up the good silver?" Mrs Hill joked. When her master did not laugh, the housekeeper knew something was wrong.

"The reason I asked you in here is simply to inform you of this message I have written. I wish for you to sign here, at the bottom. It is a formality, to show that I signed it, and this is not a forgery. When Mr Phillips returns, I will have him redo the paper, but in the meantime, I wish to have all my ducks in a row."

The butler, Mr Holly, frowned. "Is something wrong, Mr Bennet?"

"Mr Jones has apprised me that my health is not the best. With my heir away from the estate, I would prefer to make everything clear, just in case."

Mrs Hill and Mr Holly signed on the bottom of the parchment, though neither read what was written above. After they signed their names, they watched Mr Bennet place the parchment in the safe, locking it away. He handed the key to Mrs Hill, who had kept the key hidden in her office.

The day before Mr Bennet collapsed, Mrs Hill had received word that her sister had taken a fall and was injured. The lady left Longbourn, planning to take a week to assist her sister. She had just arrived the morning before Elizabeth arrived home. Having noticed someone had rummaged through her office during her absence, Mrs Hill had been suspicious. Fortunately, she located the key to the safe, securely hidden where she had placed it. What reason would Mr Collins have for looking underneath the rug which was partially under her desk?

Quietly, Mrs Hill stole away from the house at Longbourn, making her way to Netherfield Park.

~~~~~~~ ** ~~~~~~~

Chapter 14

"Mrs Darcy, you have a visitor. A Mrs Hill." The footman at Netherfield announced at the door of the drawing room.

"Mrs Hill, oh please, send her in." Elizabeth was pleased to have a chance with the lady who had aided in raising her. As the woman entered the room, Elizabeth hurried towards her, arms stretched wide.

"Hill, oh, it is wonderful to have a chance to speak. But why did you come all the way here? Has something happened?"

"Miss Lizzy, my dear girl, I have missed you. It pleases me that you have been returned to us. But I must tell you some information which will be important."

"What has happened?" Elizabeth asked, as her husband walked over to stand behind her.

"I overheard your mother and that horrid creature speaking this morning. They know that what they are doing is wrong, that your brother's birth eliminated the entail, and that Mr Collins has no rightful claim to the estate. And your mother has been assisting him, as she wishes to never have to leave Longbourn. She is trying to convince Mr Collins to marry Miss Jane, as she feels this will allow her to remain living as she has since becoming Mistress of Longbourn. But Mr Collins is adamant that he wishes to marry you. He has written to his patroness, a Lady Catherine, I believe. He feels she will be able to assist him in getting your marriage annulled."

"Mrs Hill, please know, no matter what else happens, I will never allow my marriage to be annulled." William stated. "I love this woman, and she is my wife, for the rest of my life."

"This is good news, Sir. I am pleased for my dear girl." Mrs Hill stood with her arms surrounding the young lady who meant so much to the housekeeper. "Now, I have another piece of news. Your uncle, Mr Phillips, was away before I left to take care of my sister, Frieda. Mr Bennet had Mr Holly and me sign a document he had written, as his witness. I am not certain what the document said, but he locked it in his safe. Something was said about it probably not being necessary, but he wished to be prepared."

"Has Mr Collins had a chance to go through the safe?" Mr Gardiner asked, coming into the room.

"No, Sir. Mr Bennet never kept the key to the safe. When he first gave the key to me, many years ago, he stated that no one would expect the key for the Master's safe not being in the Master's possession. And where I hid the key, no one knew it was there. Someone had ransaked my office, most likely looking for the key, but they did not find it." She held up the key in her hand.

"You do not know what was written on the parchment?" William asked.

Mrs Hill shook her head. "No, Sir. But he knew his health was declining. Mr Jones had been to see Mr Bennet, and said that he was having issues."

"Papa was dying?" Elizabeth gasped.

"He did not say those words, though it was the assumption I got from what he spoke. I am so sorry, Miss Lizzy. But he wished to have things done appropriately, in case something happened. With Mr Phillips tending family, and you and Master Alex visiting your uncle, your father wished to protect the estate and the family."

"We need to open the safe. The information could be just what is needed to force Mr Collins from the estate." William stated.

"What would we do with my mother?" Elizabeth asked.

Mr Gardiner shook his head. "I do not know

what we will do, though she should not be allowed to profit from her behavior. She does not deserve the right to remain with the rest of you."

"I do not wish to live with her." Elizabeth stated. "I cannot imagine having to endure her behavior every day." She turned to William, as his arms wrapped around her.

"And you never shall, my dearest. Have no fear. Between your uncles and my father, a solution can be found." William continued to soothe his wife, his hand caressing her back as he whispered endearments in her ear.

Mrs Hill was pleased to see Elizabeth and her husband. It did the housekeeper's heart good to see the girl she loved being cherished by the young man she married.

"Lizzy, I have a few suggestions, but we must see what happens in the next few days." Mr Darcy announced. "When your uncle, Mr Phillips, arrives, we will be able to determine how to approach the situation. I only wish there was a way we could obtain the papers in the safe."

"If I might make a suggestion." Mrs Hill started. "I think I know a way that will not alert the pair. Mrs Bennet is normally a late sleeper. I believe Mr Collins was sound asleep when I left the house. Perhaps, when I return there, I can keep Mr Collins busy in my office. It is far enough away from the Master's study, there would be no chance of his hearing one of you men coming in the rear entrance door of the house and making your way into the study. I can have Bessie, the maid who assists the girls, see to keeping Mrs Bennet upstairs. Mr Holly can be stationed in the hall, so he will know when it is safe for me to finish with Mr Collins."

"It is placing you in harm's way, Mrs Hill." Mr Gardiner replied.

"Do not fret, Sir. I will be fine. Besides, Mr Bennet gave me a small handgun and taught me how to use the weapon. It is kept in my desk drawer, and I have no difficulties in using the gun if needed."

"Mrs Hill, please be careful." Elizabeth said, turning her head to the elder woman. "I do not wish for any harm to come to you."

"It shant, my dear girl. Do not worry yourself."

~~ ** ~~

Mr Gardiner sent off an express to alert Mr Phillips of the situation, especially of the news from Mrs Hill. From the words the housekeeper had imparted, the men had all come to the opinion that Mr Bennet had written a codicil, incase he and his son were to perish.

Mr Darcy and William went to Longbourn with Mr Gardiner, staying hidden from view of the house. As Mrs Hill promised, Mr Holly stepped out the rear entrance door, pulling his watch out of his pocket, looking at it, then returning it to the same pocket. Then he turned and stepped back inside, leaving the door ajar.

William had determined he would be the best to enter the house, leaving his father and Elizabeth's uncle outside the rear door. He took the key which Mrs Hill had given him, and entered the room that had been dear to his wife. He could picture her, resting on the sofa, a book in her hand. The image in his mind brought a smile to his face. William looked forward to showing his dearest love the libraries at Darcy House and Pemberley.

Walking carefully, William made his way to the location of the safe, hidden by a false front, making it appear to be a drawer in a cabinet. Pulling as Mrs Hill instructed, William was able to quickly open the safe and pull the papers out. He decided not to take time to sort through them, so he scooped up all the contents of the safe, stuffing them inside a satchel he had brought with him.

A noise was heard from the second level, as

voices could be heard in argument. "I want Hill to attend me, not you, Bessie. Everytime you assist me, you make mistakes. Now, where is Hill? I demand to see her immediately."

"Mrs Hill is in her office, speaking with Mr Collins about some matters of importance." The young maid had only been with Longbourn for two months, and was completely at a loss as to how to keep the woman from going downstairs and interrupting and the situation being ruined.

"Then I will go to her." Mrs Bennet replied, pushing past the maid.

As Mrs Bennet came downstairs, an idea came to mind. She decided that she would not hold her breath of being assisted by the likes of William Collins for her future comforts. She would have a look at her husband's ledgers while the man was busy with Mrs Hill. As the lady turned and began to walk towards her husband's study, she was surprised to find Mr Holly in the hall.

"You have work to do, Mr Holly. There is no reason for you to be standing about."

"I was waiting for Mr Collins, as he asked me to be ready to speak with him after he finished with Mrs Hill." The butler was thinking fast.

"Well, there is no need for you to be lollygagging around here. Go wait for him elsewhere."

"But he was adamant that I wait here, by the study, so that he would not have to find me."

"He is not yet the Master of this house, though I am still the Mistress. When I tell you to do something, I expect my commands to be carried out. Do I make myself understood?"

As the butler was attempting to find a reason to remain at his post, the cook, Mrs Linder came hurrying towards the pair.

"Mrs Bennet, I have an urgent problem in the kitchen, and require your advice. Could you please come with me, so I might finish preparing your meal?"

Mrs Bennet was not pleased. She looked at the door to the study, then back at Mrs Linder. When her stomach began to voice its desire for food, she agreed to follow the cook to the kitchen.

As soon as they were out of sight, Mr Holly lightly rapped on the study door, letting William know that it was safe to come out. The younger Darcy moved swiftly and was soon with his accomplices outside Longbourn's main house.

The men left the estate and returned to

Netherfield Park, where they drew out the papers from the satchel.

Each of the men took a few pages and began reading. William was the one to discover the parchments for which they were looking.

"Yes, this is it, a codicil to Mr Bennet's will." William stated as he continued to read. "He wrote that his heart was weakened, and the headaches he had been having worried Mr Jones. That is the name of the apothecary, is it not?"

Elizabeth was sitting beside her husband, and she nodded her head. William continued, reading aloud. "Though my son is healthy and of proper age to take his inheritance, I feel it incumbent that I prepare this codicil for my will. Something is nagging at me, as it has the last few days, and I wish for all to be protected when I leave this world. So I leave this as my decision, if my heir, my dearest boy, preceedes me in death.

The entail was broken with my son's birth, allowing me to write my will as I pleased. But if my son should die before me, then I leave Longbourn to my eldest daughter, Miss Jane Louise Bennet. She may decide what to do with her mother, though I suggest that she send her mother to live in the cottage I purchased years ago, just for Fanny. The cottage is located four miles to the south of Meryton. I believe the distance would be enough to keep Fanny from visiting too often, especially if she does not have a carriage and horse. My wife is not the sort to walk four miles to Meryton and an extra three miles to Longbourn. So it might give my daughter the peace she deserves. The cottage has three bedrooms, though tiny, so if any of the younger girls decide to live with Fanny, there should be room. There is enough set aside to pay for two servants for the cottage. I pray my daughter has the strength to refrain from giving in to Fanny's demands for more.

My second eldest daughter, Miss Elizabeth Rose Bennet, is to inherit my books. I know the books should be left with the estate, but she and Alex have been the ones to share my love of reading. They have spent many hours in the study with me, reading and discussing books. I believe these will have great value to my dearest Lizzy.

For all of my daughters, I leave behind the following sums for their dowries. Mr Phillips and Mr Gardiner are both aware of the money, as they have assisted in investing it over the years.

Jane will receive the sum of one thousand pounds, in addition to the estate.

Elizabeth will receive the sum of ten thousand

pounds, in addition to the books.

Miss Mary Ann Bennet will receive the sum of fifeteen thousand pounds.

Miss Katherine Paulette Bennet will receive the sum of fifeteen thousand pounds.

Miss Lydia Frances Bennet will receive the sum of fifeteen thousand pounds.

My wife, Mrs Frances Bennet, nee Gardiner, will receive her dowry to the tune of five thousand pounds. She will also receive one hundred pounds per annum, for the upkeep of her cottage, her servants, and for Fanny's needs.

If my son is still alive when I die, all of these measures will not be in effect, and my will is to stand as it is.

My children, I pray that you will all have long and happy lives, filled with all you wish. Marry for love, not for wealth or convenience. Though I pray that this is not read for many years, I believe it will not be as I wish. And if Alex is indeed dead before me, I caution the rest of my children to worry about your own happiness, and do not allow your mother to take your happiness from you."

The end of the codicil was signed by Thomas

Alexander Bennet, Mrs Hill, and Mr Holly.

Mr Gardiner nodded his head. "Thomas knew in his heart that he would not live long. He was always a loving father. When you children were young, he came to me and Mr Phillips to discuss a business venture. I have been overseeing it for years, and it has done well. You girls were not to know, until you married or came of age. Your mother was never to know the extent, as your father was certain she would find a way to take your shares."

Elizabeth wiped the tears that had begun to flow down her cheeks. "Papa, I wish this had not been necessary, but I am so grateful for the care you took to protect us." Her eyes drifted upwards, as if searching the ceiling for heaven.

Mrs Norton entered the drawing room, carrying a silver salver. "Mr Gardiner, there is an express for you."

Taking the message from the tray, Mr Gardiner lost no time in breaking the seal. "Ah, it is from Phillips. He is on his way here, and bringing with him a constable. It appears that Mr Collins is not at all what he seems."

Everyone turned their eyes towards Mr Gardiner. "What does he say, Uncle?"

"It seems that Mr Collins is a known gambler, and has extensive debts. He has been seen frequenting two brothels in Town. There has been an investigation into his behavior, conducted by church officials. And it appears there have been complaints from the good people of Hunsford, as he takes what he wishes from the shops, and never pays for the goods. When they tell him they will no longer allow his taking their goods, Mr Collins goes directly to Lady Catherine, lying to her about the people."

"Good heavens. My sister in law is involved in this matter?" Mr Darcy was shocked. "Knowing Catherine, she will have taken his word and treated the people of Hunsford with extreme cruelty. I must send word to her, and to Lord Matlock. This will not be a pleasant situation."

"Mrs Hill said that she overheard Mr Collins saying he had sent a letter to Lady Catherine." Elizabeth said.

"Bloody Hell, then Catherine is most likely on her way here." Mr Darcy announced. Realizing he had used profanity, he apologized to everyone.

Mr Gardiner spoke again. "Well, it appears that Netherfield will be seeing many people arriving soon. My brother in law should arrive in the next few hours."

Chapter 15

Mr Phillips arrived an hour after his express, bringing with him a constable. The men were extremely fatigued from their journey, but they were ready to deal with Mr Collins.

"There is a warrant for his arrest in Essex. It appears that the man took advantage of a young lady who lives there, while he was staying at an inn. Mr William Collins, a clergyman, had attempted to seduce a young lady working in the tea shop. When she did not willingly submit to him, he forced her into a back room, raping her. The young lady was beaten, leaving her in a terrible state. It was fortunate that she survived, or there would be a murder charge against him. The man was identified by one of the shopkeepers across from the tea shop, who saw Mr Collins leave just moments before the young lady was found." Mr Phillips said, the repulsion he felt was great.

"And we have news for you." Mr Gardiner stated, as he informed the newcomers of Mr Bennet's codicil.

"Thank the stars, Thomas was prepared." Mr Phillips exhaled in relief.

"Yes, and he even knew how Fanny would behave."

"That was a sure bet, as Fanny has always thought of herself first and formost." Mrs Phillips had joined the group. She was disgusted with her sister's behavior.

"Well, I see nothing to prevent us from making our way to Longbourn." Mr Darcy looked about at the rest of the group. Everyone else was nodding their heads in agreement.

Soon, they were all loaded in carriages or on horseback. And the lives of Mrs Bennet and William Collins would never be the same.

~~ ** ~~

Mrs Hill opened the door and ushered in the large group of people. She decided not to announce them, and to allow the occupants of the parlor to be surprised. They had just been served their tea and biscuits when they were interrupted.

"See here, what is the meaning of this?" Mr Collins demanded. "How dare you barge into my home?"

"This is not your home, Mr Collins. And it never shall be yours. We have several issues to discuss with you and Mrs Bennet." Mr Phillips took the lead. "But, before we go further, I wish to introduce you to Constable Hendricks, who has come from Essex to speak with you."

Everyone could see Mr Collins turning white. "I have never been to Essex, why would a constable from there wish to speak to me?"

"Are you not Mr William Collins, who stayed at the Iron Wheel inn, three months ago? From the sketch they had circulated, I would believe that the man they are seeking is you." Mr Gardiner held forth a sketch of the wanted man.

Mrs Bennet took the paper and gasped. She instantly recognized the man in the sketch was the man sitting next to her. "Mr Collins, what is the meaning of this? It says you are wanted for violating a young lady."

"I did no such thing. I have women throw themselves at me frequently. It would be foolish to pass up something volunteered with great passion."

"And you beat young ladies who throw themselves at you?" Constable Hendricks inquired. "The young lady, Miss Lucy Fielding, was nearly beaten to death. If it had not been for the physican being nearby when Miss Fielding was found, you would be facing murder charges."

"I do not know of what you are speaking. Now, I will ask you to leave here immediately. I wish to speak with Mrs Bennet with regards to our dinner."

"Mr Collins, not only will you be leaving with Constable Hendricks, you will never inherit the estate. We have a codicil that Mr Bennet wrote, in the unfortunate possibility that his son died. The estate would then be inherited by my niece, Miss Jane Bennet." Mr Phillips spoke with disdain.

"I told you to marry Jane." Mrs Bennet shook her finger at the man. "If you had listened to me, you would be the Master of Longbourn, but no, you refused. You could only think of Elizabeth's curves. This is all your fault, you selfish man." She pulled back her hand, bringing it forward to connect with Mr Collins' cheek.

Fortunately for Mrs Bennet, Mr Darcy and William moved quickly to restrain her, while the constable and Mr Phillips moved to stop Mr Collins from retaliating.

The pair were separated, and Mr Collins was shackled, before removing him to the carriage still sitting outside the front door of the house.

Mrs Bennet decided to make good with her daughters, so as to keep her home. "Jane, my dear girl, you are such a good daughter. With your inheriting the estate, I will never have to fret about losing my home."

"Forgive me, Mamma, but I beg to differ. You have two options for your future." Jane was determined to keep control of the situation. "Papa purchased a cottage near the Long's estate. You can live there for the remainder of your life, with the provisons Papa put in place, or you can accept my dowry funds to move to America. It is your choice, but remember, you will never be allowed to remain in my home."

"B..but...but...this is not fair. I deserve to live here. How dare you, you little ingrate. After all I have done for you, that you would turn your back on me in my hour of need." Mrs Bennet was furious. "I am certain your precious Lizzy put you up to such a scheme. You can make your own mind up, there is no reason to do as your sister says."

"I made my own decision, Mamma, after the advice of Papa."

"There was no such advice in his will." Mrs Bennet pouted.

"The codicil was in his safe, signed just days

before Papa collapsed. And we are well aware of the fact that you or Mr Collins attempted to find the key for the safe. Fortunately, you never found where the key was hidden."

~~ ** ~~

Elizabeth Darcy guided her husband to the Bennet family cemetery, found near the Longbourn chapel. William was carrying a basket, as his wife had decided to give her father a final gift.

As they entered the plot of earth where Elizabeth's family had been interred for centuries, she saw the area that had been recently dug. She could feel the tears welling up in her eyes. The marker was a temporary one, until the headstone could be engraved.

Kneeling down beside the marker, running her fingers over the letters carved in it. "Papa, I survived. I returned home. You and Alex are together again. I miss you both so much."

William reached out his hand, placing it on his wife's shoulder. Elizabeth reached up and placed her hand over his. "Papa, this is Fitzwilliam Darcy. He is my husband. How I wish you were here, to meet him. You would love him, cherish the fact that he saved my life, and that he loves me. He is a good man, Papa, the best man I know. I am truly blessed."

"I wish I had been blessed to meet you, Mr Bennet, as your daughter has informed me we share a great love of reading, and we both cherish her. It is my regret that I could not save your son that day, as we boarded the ship. My cousin and I reached out, but we were not fast enough. I pray that he did not suffer, and that he is at your side, once again."

Wiping tears from her cheeks with one hand, Elizabeth reached over for the basket her husband was holding. She opened the lid and reached inside, pulling out a plant. "This is foxglove. Papa loved foxglove blooms, as he found them elegant. And foxglove is used in a tincture for heart conditions. His father used the tincture for his heart, and Mrs Hill stated that Papa had recently obtained a bottle from Mr Jones. The Latin name for foxglove is Digitalis purpurea, which digitalis comes from the digitanus, meaning finger, for the thimble shaped flowers look as if you could fit your finger inside. My grandfather used to say that there is a legend that the faeries taught foxes to ring the foxglove bells, warning each other of hunters approaching."

"That is an interesting, my dearest." Darcy knelt beside her, beginning to make a place on the grave to place the foxglove plant.

"Now, Papa's grave will call out to the faeries. They will bring magic to the estate."

Once the plant was in the ground, the couple bid a farewell to Mr Thomas Bennet.

~~ ** ~~

Epilog

Five years later

Mr Darcy was thrilled to be visiting Netherfield Park. He had purchased the estate, a wedding gift for his son and his bride. As it would be their home when visiting her relations, it also gave the couple privacy in their early years of marriage.

The privacy was appreciated by William and Elizabeth Darcy. Not long after everything had been settled in Hertfordshire, the young couple learned they would be parents. This thrilled all, but especially Gerald Darcy and Klarissa Fitzwilliam. Both were overjoyed to have a grandchild to indulge. After the birth of the next Darcy heir, Master Bennet Alexander Darcy, it was not long before the couple was once again, expecting an addition to the family.

In the five years, the Darcys had four children, with a set of twin girls born a little less than a year after Bennet. The newest member of the Darcy family was a boy, only ten months old. There was a belief that Elizabeth might be with child again, as their family speculated at every gathering. It was well known that the couple shared a bed every night, and many stories were told by the staff of the young Darcys being caught in compromising situations in many of the rooms of Netherfield.

During a visit to his friend, at Netherfield, Charles Bingley was introduced to Miss Jane Bennet. It did not take long for the young man to begin courting his "angel", as he was known to call her. They had married two years prior, and were expecting their first child any day. The couple lived at Longbourn, where they looked after the younger sisters of the Bennet family. Charles had an unmarried sister, Caroline, but she refused to visit Hertfordshire, as she felt it was too far beneath her to be in such a rustic place, where no men of high society would be found.

Mary Bennet had met a clergyman who fell in love with the young lady who preferred reading sermons to any other sort of books. They were engaged to wed in another month.

Kitty and Lydia had their coming out the previous year. Without their mother to influence them, the twins had taken their cues from their elder sisters. They were still unmarried, though the idea of a hasty marriage to a dashing officer of the militia, sporting a red coat, was no longer a temptation to them. They had come a long way in the five years.

Little Thomas was indeed thriving, and was raised alongside the Darcy children. He even referred to William as his papa and Elizabeth as his mamma. It had been decided that the boy would be given a proper education and assisted in finding a profession he would like when he was old enough.

Richard had joined the regulars, as he planned, and built his career from a lowly sergant to the rank of colonel. He worked closely with the contacts he had made in the underground network in Europe, as well as with the King's German Legion. The journey through Austria, Prussia, and Germany had boosted Richard's ability to strategize for attacks. This made Richard a valuable member of His Majesty's Army.

Klarissa and Henry Fitzwilliam were frequent guests at Netherfield Park. Though she was not the grandmother of the Darcy children, she loved them as if they were. Being with the children gave her pleasure and brought joy to her life. The Fitzwilliams also kept in close contact with those who had been on the fateful trip that saved many lives.

Erik and Margit settled down at Netherfield. William had offered Erik the position of blacksmith, and the couple was pleased to accept. Their relations in England visited, until William offered them positions as tenants at Netherfield. One of Erik's brothers had joined the King's German Legion and was a translator for Richard and his unit. The children were all grateful to the Darcy and Fitzwilliam families, especially Liam, who was given an education. He was preparing to enter the university in a few months, something of which his family would never have dreamed if they had remained in Europe. As a gift to him, his Oma gave him a set of clothing she had hand sewn. She would never forget how her grandson had acted to protect his family and the others, as they escaped Hannover. His courage had given her strength to keep alive.

Trich and Emily were able to join their family, though it was not long before they made their way to Netherfield, as a position to be tenants became available.

Mr Collins was taken to Essex, where he was positively identified by the young lady he had attacked. He was hung, leaving behind him a long list of people to whom he owed money. Lady Catherine de Bourgh was extremely displeased with the truth, as she had found the man to be impeccable. It was only after she learned that some of her belongings were found in his possessions, did the lady realize she had been bamboozled. Though she was displeased with her nephew marrying someone other than her daughter, Lady Catherine did not wish to have people learn how she had been taken in by Mr Collins. So she kept her mouth shut when it came to Mr and Mrs Fitzwilliam Darcy.

As for Mrs Bennet, well, the lady put up quite a fit when she was forced to leave Longbourn. She lived alone, in her cottage, for nearly a year, before deciding that she deserved better. So she sold the cottage and left the area, telling everyone that she would not tolerate the treatment of her ungrateful children. The last anyone had heard of the lady, she was living in Ireland, with a man she had met shortly after arriving there. They married and moved to his small estate. She refused to coorespond with her daughters and her siblings.

A letter arrived nearly six months after the fateful day in Vienna, from Randolph Gardiner. He had been able to rescue Alex's body from the river, and laid his nephew's body in the grave, next to his beloved wife. They had heard from Mr Gardiner over the years since, but none in the family had seen him since that day.

So comes the end of our tale. It was a difficult time, and much to endure, but the changes that were made in so many lives was tremendous. After the birth of the twins, Elizabeth started a journal, in which she wrote the journey to return to England. On the first page, Elizabeth wrote the following: This is the tale of the Darcys continental escape. If it had not been for that fateful day in Vienna, who knows where life would have taken them.

~~ ** ~~

THE END

ABOUT THE AUTHOR

Melanie Schertz was born and raised in central Illinois, before moving to Salt Lake City, Utah in the mid 80's. She has a Bachelor's Degree in forensics with a minor in photography, which she used as a crime lab/crime scene technician for the police for 15 years.

She fell in love with Jane Austen's stories in 2005, and finally took the plunge in 2012, publishing her first JAFF book, A Stitch of Life. Since then, she has written 23 more books, all JAFF. She is a proud member of Austen Authors and DarcyandLizzy.com.

Melanie is a mom and grandma, with both human and furry children and grandchildren.

All of Melanie's books can be found on Amazon.com. She can be found on Facebook under Melanie A Schertz (Author page) and on www.melschertz.com

Recommended by Author Melanie Schertz

COMING SOON:
from Rose Fairbanks

Sufficient Encouragement

Chapter One

Escaping the rooms of Netherfield, Elizabeth Bennet hurried to a path out of sight from the house. She intended to pick some of the last of the flowers in the nearby garden for Jane. Mr. Bingley had provided plenty of hot-house flowers for her, but Elizabeth needed a reason to escape the other residents of the house. That all but Mr. Bingley wanted her away from them was very evident.

Pushing all unpleasant thoughts from her mind, she happily cut the last blooms of mid-November in solitude until she heard the voices of Miss Bingley and Mr. Darcy. A sly smile crept across Elizabeth's face. Were they out for a lover's stroll?

"I hope you will give your mother-in-law a few hints, when this desirable event takes place, as to the advantage of holding her tongue."

Elizabeth was surprised to overhear them discuss their marriage, nor did she know Mrs. Bingley lived. More importantly, she had not seen any sign of partiality on

Darcy's behalf, but then people often married for reasons other than affection.

Miss Bingley had continued speaking. "And cure the younger girls of running after officers."

Elizabeth furrowed her brows in confusion. Miss Bingley was certainly not Mr. Darcy's intended then, and it sounded like...

"Endeavour to check that little something that borders on conceit and impertinence in your lady."

Of whom could they possibly be speaking? Elizabeth was loath to admit it, but she found eavesdropping on Mr. Darcy's conversations most fascinating. She attempted to crouch behind a bush to hear more without detection.

"Have you anything else to propose for my domestic felicity?" he coolly inquired.

"Oh yes! Do let the portraits of your aunt and uncle Phillips sit next to your great-uncle the judge. They are in the same profession, you know, only different lines. As for your Elizabeth's likeness, you must not have it taken, for who could do justice to those remarkable eyes?"

Perhaps other ladies would blush or tremble at hearing Mr. Darcy admired them, but Elizabeth saw it all as only a cruel joke. She almost missed Mr. Darcy's reply.

"It would not be easy indeed to catch the expression, but their colour and shape and the eyelashes, so remarkably fine, might be copied."

Elizabeth's eyes widened in disbelief. Mr. Darcy truly admired her? She was so uncomprehending that she could hardly guess who was alarmed more at the unexpected but inevitable meeting. Elizabeth nearly tumbled over. Throwing her arms out, she steadied herself and caught her breath.

"Miss Eliza! I had no idea you were out for a walk."

Recovering quickly, Elizabeth replied, "Oh, I was only gathering a posy for Jane."

"How does she do this morning?" Mr. Darcy politely inquired.

"She is improving quickly, thank you."

"And have you no intention of walking, then?" Darcy asked.

At the same moment, Miss Bingley spoke. "Oh, I do hope she recovers soon."

They both coloured, and Elizabeth hid her smile.

Miss Bingley began again. "Louisa and I were planning to visit dear Jane after I returned indoors."

Elizabeth smiled. "She would like that, thank you."

Darcy turned to Miss Bingley. "Why not visit with her now? It would allow Miss Bennet a more ample excursion. She has scarcely left her sister's side, and the exercise would do her well."

"Oh yes. Why, of course. Do excuse us, Miss Elizabeth." She began to turn but ceased when Darcy did not follow her. "Mr. Darcy, I had thought you were returning as well."

Elizabeth turned her face to avoid laughing at the suspicion of desperation in Miss Bingley's voice.

"No, you know I always indulge in an hour's exercise in the morning."

Miss Bingley begrudgingly returned to the house, and Elizabeth hoped Darcy would return to his walk.

"Do you not feel a great inclination for a country walk?"

She lightly laughed at his request; his words mirrored the ones he spoke the night before when he asked her for a reel. She took his arm as they began to walk away from the house.

"My, my, Mr. Darcy. Hertfordshire is rubbing off on you! First you want to dance a reel, and now a country walk instead of on the avenue of sculpted gardens?"

He smiled. "I miss the wilds of Derbyshire."

"You do not spend much time in Town?"

"My estate requires much of my attention, but I make trips to Town as often as I can. My sister resides mostly in London for the masters, so it is natural I would wish to spend time with her."

A single young man of rank and wealth enjoying London only to spend time with his sister? "The amusements of Town do not compel you?"

"I enjoy the diversions of the theatre and the like, particularly the access to the bookshops, but cannot care for all the people."

Of course, he could not, for most of them were beneath his notice. "Cannot or will not?"

"You imply I do not converse easily with people out of choice."

"Easily? I daresay you do not converse with anyone outside your own party."

"I am speaking to you."

He gave her a pointed look, and Elizabeth grew troubled as she considered again the words she heard earlier. "I suppose you have found some amusement in speaking with me because you have made it clear you dislike talking with the others from the area."

She glanced up at him, and indeed, he did look amused.

"You think you have my character entirely sketched, then? And on only a few weeks' acquaintance when, by your own testament, I barely speak?"

She had thought that exactly, that is until a moment ago. She could not admit such a thing, though.

"I mean no offence when I say some characters are easier to sketch than others."

He laughed lightly, and it was as though the sun broke through the clouds on his face. Why would such a handsome man wish to appear grim so often?

"You are uncommonly clever, Miss Bennet."

She tried to contain her surprise. A compliment from Mr. Darcy?

She was silent too long, and his voice close to her ear startled her. "The correct response would be to thank me."

She blushed. No, of course, he would not mean to praise her. It was only a means to criticise her again.

"I apologise. I was searching for the correct response to that particular kind of compliment."

"I did not know compliments came in different forms."

"Oh, but they do. If at a ball I say how beautiful one's headdress looks and how delicate it is, and it would be a shame to see it suffer ill-effects, you may be sure I am not complimenting the lady on her ability to dance but rather suggesting she sit out."

A small smile crept across his face. "And what kind of compliment was my praise?"

She looked down at her feet. "Perhaps you find that I am too intelligent for a woman. Perhaps any intelligence from those of my sex takes you by surprise. Perhaps, from one with such decided opinions on what makes an accomplished lady, you were truly pointing out what you conceive as a failure of mine."

Satisfied she had made perfect sense of his earlier praise and that he could not be offended by her seeing through his *façade*, she left his side after exclaiming at the sight of wildflowers. When he approached her, she raised her eyebrows in expectation. Regardless of what he thought of her intelligence, she was sincerely beginning to doubt his.

"You claimed I conceived your intelligence a failure..."

She quickly interrupted him. "Yes, because I am sure the rest of the world does not have such ridiculous expectations." Actually, she was not so certain at all. She knew Meryton did not.

"True, I do have high expectations. I am certain the rest of society, who enjoy the frivolousness of *soirée*s and gambling, cannot possibly value a lady who is well read and entertains independent thoughts."

Elizabeth was quick to reply. "Undoubtedly, no lady who has so much intelligence and sense would also kill herself to become accomplished in languages, art, dancing, conversation, and everything else you and Miss Bingley believe are required of a woman. Any lady of sense would not go through all that simply for the label of accomplishment and to be displayed on some man's arm. A woman with so much talent and intelligence would pursue study out of enjoyment and self-gratification and would have too much self-respect to marry only to be an ornament."

"Then we are in agreement on what an accomplished lady is like."

Elizabeth raised her eyebrows in disbelief. His words reminded her of something she overheard on the day of her arrival at Netherfield. "Do you also think being thus accomplished makes a woman a more attractive marital partner?"

He answered cautiously, "Many gentlemen would pursue a lady with so much sense and ability."

"Gentlemen of sense may think so. Alas, there has been a shortage of gentlemen of sense in my acquaintance. I often meet with men who believe an alliance should be based on connections and fortune."

Darcy smiled a little. "Are you now to give me a list of what is required for a gentleman?"

"Perhaps you are not the only one with exacting standards. To me, the perfect gentleman is amiable to all he meets and puts his feelings and desires last. He considers those in his care as his primary concern. Perhaps this gives him little time to read or write long letters. He takes care only to have friends of the greatest sense, and so he may rely upon their advice."

Her companion frowned. "You return to our subject from last night. My friend is unaffectedly modest, and he does rely on my advice perhaps too greatly. I hope I meet with his demands of having good sense. But do you not make allowances for differences in temper and situation? Bingley is very obliging to everyone he meets, and he cannot imagine an offence against him. To assume that I am less gentlemanly than him only because I cannot forgive all the crimes against me would be as if I believed you less of a lady than those who do not walk three miles to nurse their sister or those who defer to every opinion spoken by a gentleman. You give my sex no compliment by believing we must all have the same temperament."

"I speak as I find."

"And do you still agree that you do not meet as many people with differing personalities in the country?"

"I suppose I must."

"Then perhaps you have not met many gentlemen who can disprove your narrow constraints of gentlemanly behaviour."

"Logic would follow that would be the case, and yet you, in all your broad acquaintance, have not met more than half a dozen ladies who are truly accomplished."

He was silenced, and Elizabeth smiled to herself. Now no one could say she recommended herself to the other sex by undervaluing her own. She rather thought little of men.

"I ought to return to Jane. I have gathered enough flowers."

She turned to leave and was rather amazed when he continued to follow. She had believed he was affronted by her words.

"I have been thinking," he began, "on your words about the influence of friendship."

"For all that I argued that one of an amiable temper might quickly change his decision out of regard for the friend, you will not change my opinion, sir."

He chuckled. "I would not dream of it."

Elizabeth laughed in return. "How diplomatic of you! For, by your agreement, you either state we are not friends or that I do not have an amiable temper."

"Perhaps I believe this to be too important a subject to try to turn your opinion."

She was not sure how to reply.

"I have been thinking that one could benefit from the affection of a good friend."

She ought not to be surprised. She overheard him declare he admired her, but still the idea that he spoke of it stopped her in her tracks. She silently waited for him to continue.

"I have a sister who is more than ten years my junior. She was taken from school last spring. Her education was completed, but she has missed having friends."

She blushed. How silly of her! Had she thought he would declare love for her in Mr. Bingley's garden? "I had thought Miss Bingley and Mrs. Hurst quite friendly with her."

"I believe she may value ones closer to her age and of a certain, shall we say more benevolent, disposition. Might I persuade you and your eldest sister to strike up a correspondence with her?"

She began to argue, but he anticipated her reasons. "I am uncertain how long I will remain in the country, and if I would ever bring her here, it would be nice for her to have more acquaintances."

They reached the house just before then, and Elizabeth dislodged her arm as she flushed. "Certainly, sir. Thank you for the escort."

"My pleasure."

After a bow and a curtsy, she fled his side for Jane's room. Miss Bingley and Mrs. Hurst were sitting with Jane and stared daggers at her. Thankfully, they quickly made their excuses. Certainly they perceived Mr. Darcy had returned, and so Jane could be of little interest to them then.

Jane soon rested, and Elizabeth was left with her thoughts. She had seldom had an admirer before. Frowning, she considered that the ones she did have in the past did not seem to keep their attention on her long—if they noticed her at all instead of Jane. Not that she had wanted to encourage any of the gentlemen. Indeed, she had no wish to encourage Mr. Darcy for whatever distraction he provided.

Then she reconsidered. Mr. Darcy had argued even the night before how easily led Mr. Bingley was. Undoubtedly, Mr. Darcy had influence over his friend. If she spurned him, his pride would demand he leave Netherfield. Would he take his friend with him? Jane deserved every chance with Mr. Bingley!

Jane was not only Elizabeth's closest sister; she was her closest confidante as well. She believed Mr. Bingley held Jane's heart. Believing highly in the connection and value of her family, Elizabeth usually accepted and overlooked flaws in her relations that she would not dismiss as readily for many others. Still, Elizabeth knew how they appeared to the proud guests at

Netherfield Park. Already she felt that the wildness of her youngest sisters, coupled with her mother's ridiculousness and unabashed chastisement of Mr. Darcy, put a connection to her family in a poor light. How terrible it would be if Jane's hopes were to be disappointed by the work of her nearest kin.

Elizabeth's mind quickly flicked from her mother and sisters to herself. She had often delighted in sparring with Mr. Darcy in an attempt to put him down. Her own behaviour could just as easily cost Jane's happiness as anyone else's. If she could persuade him that a match between his friend and her sister was not an evil, then she would simply have to temper her own behaviour and swallow the discomfort. Obviously, Mr. Darcy could never mean anything serious by his admiration. Elizabeth had overheard her family and relations mocked by Mr. Darcy and Miss Bingley on more than one occasion before he admitted finding her pretty. Just now he did not act the part of a lover at all. Admiration did not a proposal make.

*****

After the men had their port and cigars, Darcy arrived in the drawing room with a feeling of trepidation. Walking with Elizabeth this afternoon had been a treat, but he gave her too much notice, and Miss Bingley was certainly aware. He could ill afford to raise Elizabeth's expectations. He would adhere to his book this evening and not fall for any of her enchanting conversation.

Thus, the feeling of panic when he saw Miss Bennet down from her room betrayed his true feelings. If she was well enough to leave her room soon, she would be well enough to leave for Longbourn, and then... No. It mattered not.

Elizabeth was at work, and he quelled the urge to watch her nimble fingers, instead applying himself to his book. Miss Bingley selected the second volume of the very book he read and attempted to ask all manner of questions, but he returned to his book after every inquiry. Eventually, thankfully, she tossed her book aside and instead asked Elizabeth to walk about the room with her.

He blinked back his surprise at the request. His eyes refused his commands to ignore her as he studied Elizabeth at Miss Bingley's side. He had always found Elizabeth pretty and was captivated by her eyes, especially within a few meetings, but this evening she looked truly lovely. He knew she ought to look tired, but he believed their walk this morning did her well. There was something unexpectedly becoming about her gown or hair arrangement. As a man, he paid little attention to such things, but he felt this was not the same lady who cared so little for their good opinion that she arrived with dirty petticoats and unkempt hair.

"Will you not join us, Mr. Darcy?" Miss Bingley asked.

Suddenly aware that he had closed his book and could not use it as an excuse, he blurted out the first thing he could think of: something about them only having two motives for walking about the room in such a way. Truthfully, he barely knew half of what flew out of his mouth when Elizabeth was near, and others were scrutinizing him in the room.

Miss Bingley was insistent on understanding his meaning, and fortunately, he had recovered his wits. Elizabeth accused him of meaning to be severe on them, so naturally he must argue the opposite.

"I have not the smallest objection to explaining them," he said as soon as she allowed him to speak. "You either choose this method of passing the evening because you are in each other's confidence and have secret affairs to discuss, or because you are conscious that your figures appear to the greatest advantage in walking; if the first, I would be completely in your way, and if the second, I can admire you much better as I sit by the fire."

He tried not to betray his thoughts that he very much wished they would walk by the fire; the light might catch more of the outline of Elizabeth's superb figure. She blushed at his words, but Miss Bingley clearly believed such a compliment was due the entire time. Would he ever be free of that woman?

Miss Bingley said Darcy deserved punishment, and Elizabeth suggested they all laugh at each other. Did she truly believe him incapable of finding amusement in things? He had smiled and laughed unguardedly with her this morning.

When Miss Bingley declared that Mr Darcy could never be laughed at, Elizabeth demurred, "Mr. Darcy is not to be laughed at! That is an uncommon advantage, and uncommon I hope it will continue, for it would be a great loss to me to have many such acquaintances. I dearly love a laugh."

"Miss Bingley," said he, "has given me more credit than can be. The wisest and the best of men—nay, the wisest and best of their actions—may be rendered ridiculous by a person whose first object in life is a joke." This was not what he wanted to say at all! He enjoyed Elizabeth's laughter. Why must he unconsciously reach for defence in her presence?

"Certainly," replied Elizabeth, "there are such people, but I hope I am not one of them. I hope I never ridicule what is wise and good. Follies and nonsense, whims and inconsistencies, they do divert me, I own, and I laugh at them whenever I can. But these, I suppose, are precisely what you are without."

"Perhaps that is not possible for anyone. But it has been the study of my life to avoid those weaknesses that often expose a strong understanding to ridicule."

If his eyes would not obey his intentions, then neither would his mouth. He wished he could flirt or converse easily as he had often seen Bingley do. As Bingley did do in the corner with Jane Bennet. Instead, he resigned himself for Elizabeth's counter to skewer him with her sharp wit. He certainly set himself up for it. What would she find in him to ridicule? And why did he welcome her criticism? Perhaps it was only the excitement of having a pretty and new acquaintance's attention to himself.

She cocked her head as she thought. "You dislike dancing, I assume, as you did not stand up with anyone outside your party at the assembly last month. Nor did you eagerly attend to the dance floor at Lucas Lodge. Yet when prompted by the correct person, you are amenable to dancing. Indeed, with certain tunes it seems you can even desire a set on your own. I begin to think it is perfectly fitting for dancing to be your moment of folly and whim."

Was she flirting with him? "Perhaps the inducement is only the correct partner," he whispered lowly, even to his ears.

Miss Bingley and Elizabeth both gasped quietly. He had been far too direct.

Miss Bingley hastily said, "Speaking of dancing, I should very much like to hear you play something, Miss Elizabeth. I recall your performance at Lucas Lodge; what a lovely piece you played."

Darcy understood her motivation. The piece would be conducive to dancing, and Miss Bingley sought to trap him with a set.

"Thank you, but I would hate to perform the same piece to the same audience, and you have such a lovely selection. Could you show me some of the Italian ones?"

Miss Bingley coldly agreed and retreated. As Elizabeth walked behind, she cast a look over her shoulder at Darcy.

"Allow me to turn the pages for you," he heard himself say as he followed her.

"Oh, that is really not necessary. Read your book, and I will turn for Miss Eliza," Miss Bingley bit out.

Darcy repressed a sigh at the sacrifice to be paid, but it would be worth it. "But if you do, then you will not have time to select your piece. Miss Bennet did not get to hear your superior performance last night."

Seemingly pleased with the compliments, she agreed and left him and Elizabeth in peace. As Miss Bingley selected her song, her eyes frequently fell upon them. Elizabeth sang sweetly, and as he leaned in with each page, he could not help but to inhale her scent.

He noticed the rosiness of Elizabeth's smooth cheeks. Wondering if his presence affected her, he allowed himself just barely to brush her side on one occasion. He would have felt like a cad but for the sound of her breath catching.

Alas, much too soon her piece was finished, and he resigned himself to his penance of turning pages for Miss Bingley and Mrs. Hurst. More than once, however, he was reprimanded for his straying attention. He sought Elizabeth's eyes across the room. She sat talking to her sister and Bingley; her eyes brightened with amusement.

Upon reaching his room that evening, he realised he would have to make some resolve about Elizabeth. He was paying her too much attention for a mere acquaintance. His mind told him of his danger, but a bigger part of him was too excited to care. It was...thrilling to be in her presence, and he had never felt such a wonderful feeling before.

Coming Soon
from Gianna Thomas

Darcy Chooses By Gianna Thomas

Chapter XXXV The next morning Darcy broke his fast and then rode out on Windstorm. He noted that the grass seemed drier than other summers and the crops presented the same dry appearance. If the rains didn't come soon, many of the crops might be lost. That afternoon he was to meet with his steward, and he would emphasize how important it was for the tenants and all the residents to avoid any trash burning or any fires other than those for cooking food that should be done only indoors. No outdoor fires of any kind would be tolerated until they had rain and no chance of an accidental conflagration. Later in his study, while finishing some correspondence, he heard someone yelling his name—for the second time in less than a week—from the front of the house. Darcy jumped up and started running toward the door.

Ned Stone had all but shoved Reynolds out of the way when the butler opened the entry to Pemberley.

"Mr. Darcy! Mr. Darcy! Fire! Fire! There's a grass fire down at Ken Johnson's place."

Darcy had darted out of his study at Stone's shouts. "Has Benjamin Driscoll been alerted?"

"Yes, sir. He and his men are already hitching the horses to all the water wagons. They're also wetting down blankets and gathering the gunpowder. Everything else is ready, but the wind has increased, and the fire is spreading fast."

Darcy's worst nightmare was being realized. "Bloody hell! Everything is extremely dry after no rain for eight weeks. Johnson's place is not that far from Kympton either. Is the fire headed that direction?" "Slowly, sir. However, the wind is blowing from the north, northeast, and the fire is rapidly heading for Lambton."

"We'll need the gunpowder for additional firebreaks. Hopefully, we can head it off in time. Are the horses saddled?"

"Windstorm and the others, sir."

"Good man. Give me five minutes to change clothes, and we'll join the water wagons. Reynolds, alert the male servants and have them meet us at the stables." "Yes, sir."

Six years earlier a grass fire had prompted Gerald Darcy to have fire wagons, that would be horse drawn, to be built and kept ready in case of another devastating fire. Draft horses with strength and speed—trained to tolerate fire and smoke—were purchased that were capable of pulling the fully loaded wagons. These were outfitted with steam engines that had the ability to shoot water through leather hoses to spray on any fire. Men were hired to keep the animals and equipment prepared for fires in the future with the men periodically training and learning how to fight any outbreaks. Old Darcy had been determined to not let fire threaten the tenants, their livings or his own home, Pemberley, ever again. What happened that day would prove whether or not his forward thinking would yield good results as they were currently under the first real threat of any size for several years.

As Stone and Darcy, along with most of the male servants, raced toward the stables, Darcy asked what had started the fire.

"Johnson was burning trash behind his place when the wind picked up. He and his family got away safely but his house is gone."

"Blasted idiot. That's why no trash was to be burned until we had rainfall."

Ordinarily, Darcy did not swear, but he found himself furious at the disregard for safety, not only to Johnson's family but anyone five to ten miles around who could be burned out.

Vaulting onto Windstorm's back, Darcy urged him into a gallop and headed toward the huge stone stables that housed the water wagons and the big draft horses. He found that Driscoll had the horses hitched to the seven water wagons, and they were all ready to move toward the main portion of the fire.

"Driscoll, did the outriders alert the tenants in the path of the fire?"

"Yes, Mr. Darcy, even the tenants north of the fire as well. And riders were sent to Kympton and Lambton to recruit more men and the towns' water wagons. The ones from Kympton will take the nearest flank and part of the back edge, and Lambton's men will take the other flank and the balance of the back edge while we take the head of the fire."

"And are your men prepared to use the gunpowder in making additional firebreaks?"

"Yes, sir. I've been having them drill with small amounts of gunpowder to get them familiar with the explosions, and they know the correct amounts to use in case of a real fire."

"Excellent, Driscoll. We'll hope that all your preparations and your men can save lives and property. Come on."

As Darcy jerked his arm over his head in a commanding gesture, men and wagons poured out of the stables and headed toward the site of the fire. Heartbeats and breathing increased as they anticipated fighting a beast—although they were prepared for it—a beast that was fear inspiring. Darcy was not the only one praying for a safe resolution to the current dilemma, hoping that it would not prove to be deadly.

A short distance, out of the path of the fire, Darcy and the other riders abandoned their horses to a number of grooms and rode the rest of the way on the water wagons. When they reached the site, they could see that the wind was picking up due to the air temperature increasing, and knew they had a fight on their hands. If they were unable to stop the wall of flames or were in danger of being caught by it, the attendants minding the horses would bring the mounts closer so the firefighters could get out of the way. As it was, they were facing a half-mile swath of a wheat crop fully engulfed that had begun when the wildfire jumped the plowed firebreak a mile back. Men from Kympton and Lambton were what were needed to fight the fire as well as any tenants who were available. Many hands would be necessary to beat the beast before it devastated the area. Catching up with Driscoll, Darcy quickly quizzed him about the distribution of the water wagons and where they could be refilled. "Five of the wagons will fight the head of the fire, and one each will sweep around and fight part of the flanks. Then we planned on taking the empty wagons to the river for refilling, sir."

"Driscoll, we need to make use of Miller's Springs, which is closer than the river. That pond has kept its level in spite of the drought. What about taking three of the wagons to the springs before they are completely empty and returning them to fight the fire before the others empty and head toward the river? Could we keep at least a few of the wagons at the fire while others replenish their supply?" "That would be much better than having all gone at the same time. I'll alert all the drivers as to the order they need to follow." With that, Driscoll ran toward the closest wagon and began giving commands to his men. In the meantime, Darcy had men hosed down to keep sparks from setting their clothes on fire. It would help, but only for a short while as the hot wind was drying their shirts and trousers rapidly. It wasn't a foolproof plan.

Darcy had been beating at the fire for about a half-hour when suddenly there was a scream from his left. Whirling he saw one of the men—whose shirt was ablaze from sparks—start running. Grabbing a wet blanket, Darcy sprinted after him and managed to tackle the man before he got too far. Wrapping him in the blanket, he began rolling him on the ground until the flames were out. "Dawson," Darcy shouted, "where's the doctor?"

"He's with the horses. I'll signal him to come over."

"Have him bring an extra horse for this man. He's burned pretty badly."

"Yes, sir." Dawson had several colored flags that could been seen at a distance, and soon two grooms and two extra horses came closer to the men. They still had to stay a short distance away from the firefighters, as the animals were skittish and hard to handle.

"Two of you men pick him up and carry him to the doctor. Move it! Now!" Darcy was impatient to get back to stopping the encroaching flames and knew they would be fortunate if they only saw one injury that day. The severely burned man was put up in front of one of the grooms—after the doctor did a quick check—and all three men left the area to Darcy's relief.

Farther ahead of the fire, Darcy spotted Driscoll and ran to him to inquire about the gunpowder and if they were ready to widen the firebreak.

"Almost, sir. We're still laying some stockpiles and fuses but should be ready in about four minutes. Make sure the men stay well away from the explosives."

Darcy told him he would see to it and began warning all the men fighting the flames in the area. Five minutes later, the explosives blew and the plowed firebreak was widened by about fifteen feet. Driscoll's men began laying more gunpowder stockpiles and fuses to increase the firebreak farther before it was jumped while Darcy and the other men continued their efforts.

***

After six hours of grueling work, the fire had been extinguished. Darcy saw that Driscoll had everything in hand, so he found one of the outriders and gave him orders to pass along to the others. These orders meant that throughout the night they would take shifts traveling the route of the fire and beyond to make sure no hot spots still existed. The semi-darkness with only a half moon would contribute to their ability to locate any and alert the firefighters who would also work in shifts. Each would grab a few hours sleep and then head out again. No one would get a full night's sleep until the fire was totally gone. Georgiana was waiting for her brother when he returned.

"William, are you all right?"

"Yes, Sweeting. Other than a few burns from sparks, I am well…and exhausted, though my clothes will need to be replaced. We were fortunate in that the many firebreaks we had helped exceedingly along with the water wagons and the many men who fought the blaze…Please tell Mrs. Reynolds I need food and a bath as well as some of her burn ointment. After bathing I'll sleep for about two hours and then return to help the outriders ensure there is no more fire. It will be a very long night."

"Are the tenants and homes safe?" his sister asked anxiously.

"Sit down, Georgie." His sister sat but with trepidation. Was something wrong? Darcy paused and determined how to tell her.

"Only three homes were lost, but several people were injured with one severely, a larger number suffered from the heat, and…there was one death."

"Oh, no! Who died?"

"The fire frightened Jenny Baker so much that her babe came early. Mrs. Baker is recuperating, but the babe was lost. The midwife...never could get the child to breathe. The Bakers, of course, are bereft."

With that, Georgiana burst into tears. "But that was her first child, and she so looked forward to it. She and her husband were both so happy. I can't imagine how sad they must be." Finally, when her tears had ceased, she sniffled and made plans to take food and some flowers to help comfort her friend. A true Darcy, she knew and loved all the tenants and their children. However, Jenny was a special friend, only three years older, and she and Georgie both had been excited about the coming babe. And now it would never be, and it broke her heart.

**

Three hours later found Darcy riding the ten-mile perimeter of his property and speaking with outriders he met along the way. Other than a small stand of trees that had caught fire and been doused, there had been no other sign that any fire lingered. When dawn came, however, the men did not stop their patrols for the next 48 hours until they were sure the fire was completely out.

Although injuries due to sparks had been minor, for the most part, Darcy made arrangements to meet with Driscoll about clothing that would help protect the firefighters. Oil cloth or clothing that was very tightly woven and waterproof might help in that regard. However, Darcy knew they had to do more to not only protect against fire in the future, they needed to protect the men's lives also. No stone would be left unturned in that regard.

**

Three days later, it rained.

Made in the USA
Middletown, DE
19 June 2022

67204041R00139